"Why did you run?" he asked with what sounded like idle curiosity.

"Why do I always run?" she replied, throwing caution to the wind-tossed sea.

"You usually run when I'm trying to seduce you. This time you seemed to run because I wasn't."

"I guess there's no pleasing me." Molly shrugged with an attempt at indifference.

"I wouldn't say that," he drawled, and the inherent promise in his voice sent shivers down her spine.

Steeling herself, she turned to meet his gaze, then wished she hadn't. The intensity in the gray depths seemed to see right through her weak defenses, and she realized that James had accomplished just what he had so obviously set out to do. He had demoralized her, turned her into someone who thought celibacy and independence a poor second to love. And she hated him for it, almost as much as she wanted him....

ABOUT THE AUTHOR

Anne Stuart began her writing career at age seven when she was first published by *Jack and Jill* magazine. Her first novel was published by the time she was twenty-five. Anne lives in rural Vermont, and lists her hobbies as quilting, reading, and daydreaming.

Books by Anne Stuart

HARLEQUIN AMERICAN ROMANCES
30-CHAIN OF LOVE
39-HEART'S EASE
52-MUSEUM PIECE

These books may be available at your local bookseller.

For a free catalog listing all titles currently available, send your name and address to:

Harlequin Reader Service
P.O. Box 52040, Phoenix, AZ 85072-2040
Canadian address: Stratford, Ontario N5A 6W2

Museum Piece

ANNE STUART

Harlequin Books

TORONTO • NEW YORK • LONDON
AMSTERDAM • PARIS • SYDNEY • HAMBURG
STOCKHOLM • ATHENS • TOKYO • MILAN

Published April 1984

ISBN 0-373-16052-6

Chapter One

"Damn him, damn him, damn him!" Mary Lindsay
McDonough, known as Molly to her father, Lindsay
to her friends, and the ambiguous M. L. McDonough
to her professional colleagues at San Francisco's Museum of American Arts, snapped a pencil in one
slender hand as she contemplated the latest disaster.
"Damn his soul to hell!"

"And who are you damning so heartily?" Lucia
Caldwell queried from the open doorway of Molly's
small elegant office on the third floor of the stately old
museum. "I'll be glad to damn his soul along with
you. My opinion of the male sex isn't particularly high
right now, and I'm more than willing to add another
name to my list of turkeys. Who's done what to
you?" Sauntering in on absurdly high heels, Lucia
slouched her thin elegant body into a chair near
Molly's antique partners' desk, the only piece of furniture large enough to hold the clutter she usually
worked with.

Molly couldn't restrain the usual sigh of admiration
and jealousy at Lucia's racehorse-slim body, and her

anger diminished, leaving her awash in depression. "How do you manage to look so good, Lucia?" she asked, distracted for the moment. "If I wore a dress like that, I'd look like a stuffed tomato."

"That's because you're blessed with hips and breasts. Not that you put them to any use, heaven knows. If I had your figure, half of the Bay Area would be at my feet."

"Instead of the current three quarters," Molly supplied cheerfully. "Don't you realize thin is in? You have the perfect figure." She looked down at her own lush curves disparagingly.

"Perfect for a broomstick. Besides, I thought you told me you accepted weighing ten pounds more now than when you were eighteen; that you were tired of starving yourself down and eating yourself back up. Didn't you throw away your designer jeans?"

"I did," Molly verified. "But that doesn't mean that I'm overjoyed by the state of things. I just decided to be realistic." She pushed a slender, ringless hand through her beautifully cut curtain of golden-blond hair, and her blue eyes were rueful. She was a fairly potent package of femininity, and well she knew it, despite her disclaimers. The unwanted ten pounds filled out her lush figure, settling quite nicely on her breasts, with an added curve to her hips. Her legs were long for her five feet six inches, and her enchanting smile, accentuated by one shy dimple, her laughing blue eyes, which filled her face, and her husky voice had all captivated more than one susceptible gentleman. Her obvious attractions only added to their frustrations as she inevitably turned them down.

"You still haven't told me who you were damning so heartily when I walked by. Do I dare hope that the mighty have fallen? Is it an *affaire de coeur*?" Lucia cooed, her brown eyes avid with interest.

"No, it is not. When I find someone to entice me from my celibacy, you'll be the first to know. He'll have to be someone quite special if I'm going to have my very pleasant life disrupted. And it certainly won't be someone like James Elliott."

"Aha! The light begins to dawn. What's Elliott done this time?"

"Snatched an absolutely beautiful dry sink that I've been chasing after for months. It was carved in the Wyoming territory in eighteen sixty and is just magnificent," she mourned. "I had just got the acquisition approved when that snake, that swine, that skunk, that despicable robber baron, stole it from me!" Her hands formed tight fists, and she searched around on her cluttered desk for another pencil to break.

"You shouldn't let it get to you, kid," Lucia said calmly. "We're a fairly well-endowed museum, but there's no way we can compete with the buying power of J. E. Seaquist behind Elliott. Seaquist's one of the ten richest men in the world, and Elliott seems to have his complete trust, at least when it comes to artistic acquisitions. You'll simply have to admit defeat and look elsewhere. It couldn't have been the only dry sink."

"It wasn't. But it was one of the best. And I'm not

about to give up. This is the third time it's happened. If he does it a few more times, I'll lose my credibility—not to mention my good nature and my sanity.''

Lucia leaned forward, her tousled brown curls framing her flushed sensual face. "Have you tried reasoning with him? Have you ever met him, as a matter of fact? He keeps a pretty low profile, just like his mysterious employer.''

"I've seen him," Molly said shortly. "Several months ago, from a distance. And I'd prefer to keep it that way.''

"But why? I've never seen a man you can't handle. First you disarm them with your wicked tongue, then you charm them with your wit and sweet common sense, and then you turn them into platonic friends.'' Lucia shook her head in wondering disgust. "I wish I could manage it. Not the platonic part, of course. But I'd like to be able to get the upper hand as easily as you manage it.''

A reluctant smile lit Molly's face. "You'll never manage, Lucia. The trick to it all is being untouchable. As long as I know that I don't have to please them, don't have to *need* them, then I'm in a position of power. If I found myself attracted to someone, all my nice control would disappear. And I'm not ready to let that happen.''

"You sound like a witch. Don't they lose their powers if they fall in love?''

"Don't all women?" Molly countered.

"What a cynic!" Lucia laughed. "It's been two years since you and Sebastian broke up. How long are you going to keep up this bloodless life?''

"It's not bloodless, it's very comfortable. I have a beautiful apartment, all to myself, where I can do what I want, when I want. I have friends to go out with, books and music to stay home with, a marvelous job, money, and independence. I like buying clothes and dressing up, just for my own pleasure and pride. Why should I trade my pleasant life for pain, uncertainty, heartbreak, and eventual despair?" She leaned back and surveyed the soothing cream-colored walls of her small office and the perfect muted tones of the Andrew Wyeth painting she'd cajoled from the museum's director. They pleased her with their perfection.

"But how long is this going to go on? This new celibacy of yours?" Lucia demanded caustically.

"Until I find a man who's worth risking everything for. And not until then." She leaned forward, pushing sheafs of papers aside until she came up with a treasure—half a box of chocolates. Popping one into her mouth, she grinned. "And how did we get back on this subject? I thought we were discussing the crimes of one James Elliott."

"I'm not so sure the subjects are far removed. In the four years I've known you, he's the only man who's managed to get the better of you. Even Sebastian couldn't manage that, no matter how hard he tried. What does he look like?"

Controlling the sudden nervous stiffening of her neck muscles, Molly answered blandly enough. "Oh, Sebastian's six and a half feet tall, massive shoulders, melting eyes, wonderful red hair, and the cutest little—"

"I wasn't talking about your ex-lover," Lucia snapped, unamused. "I saw enough of that brilliant jackass when you were living with him. I mean the mysterious James Elliott. Is he young, old, ugly, handsome, gay, macho, whatever? Come on, give forth!"

"Are you still on the lookout, Lucia?" Molly sighed with mock severity. "What happened to Jeff?"

A slow, sensuous smile curved Lucia's red-tinted mouth. "Jeff was weeks ago, darling. You're way out of date. I have to make up for your abstinence, you know. But no, I'm not interested—at least, not for me. Come on, kiddo, satisfy my raging curiosity. What's he like?"

"I saw him only from across a room, several months ago. And I would say he's none of the things you mentioned." Reaching for another chocolate, she made the supreme sacrifice and pulled back her hand, covering temptation with a pile of appraisal sheets. "He's neither terribly old nor terribly young. Somewhere in his mid-thirties, I would guess."

"The right age," Lucia noted with satisfaction. "You're thirty."

Molly cast her an unappreciative glance before continuing. "He's certainly not ugly, but I'm not sure I'd call him handsome either. He's rather thin and elegant and somewhat forbidding in an arrogant way."

"He's gay," Lucia mourned.

"I don't think so," Molly said meditatively. "Though he's certainly not your macho type—all hairy chest and bulging muscles."

"Like Sebastian."

"Like Sebastian," Molly verified. "And that's about all I know."

"Where did you meet him?"

"The usual place. Some sort of gallery cocktail party. And I didn't meet him. Someone pointed him out to me, and I took one look and ran." The moment the words were out she could have bitten her tongue at the satisfaction in Lucia's knowing brown eyes.

"You ran, eh? Now, I wonder why?"

"Because he's exactly the sort of man I keep away from. Men in suits frighten me."

"Funny, I never noticed that before."

"All right, then, damn you. James Elliott scares me. The farther away from him I can stay, the happier I'll be."

Lucia made no effort to hide her grin. "It does seem as if the mighty are about to fall. When are you going to meet him?"

"Never, if I have my way. I'm going to send him a very polite, very hostile letter informing him that if he interferes with one more of my acquisitions, I will cut his throat and slash his tires, and that should be the extent of my relationship with him. Besides, he was accompanied by Cynthia Seaquist at that cocktail party, and they looked very close. I'm certainly not about to compete with the likes of her."

"But why not? Your family doesn't quite have the Seaquist millions, but you're scarcely paupers. If you wanted him..."

Molly counted to ten, slowly, and then managed a tight smile that Lucia knew far too well. "I do not want James Elliott. I haven't even met James Elliott. The only thing I want from James Elliott is his head on the prerevolutionary pewter platter he managed to steal from under my nose last June."

A doubtful expression clouded Lucia's beautiful eyes. "You wouldn't really write him and tell him that you'll cut his throat, would you?"

A wicked grin lit Molly's face. "You don't think so?" she questioned smoothly. "How well do you know me?"

Lucia groaned. "Won't the old man bust a gut if he finds out?"

"Dr. Matheson has complete trust in me. Besides, he wanted that pewter platter even more than I did. This is a declaration of war, Lucia. Dr. Matheson will back me up if need be."

"You're probably right. If *I* told someone I'd cut his throat, I'd doubtless be fired," she complained, sighing. "Oh, well, I guess I'm just as glad I'm only a minor assistant curator, rather than one of the official assistants to the curator. Even if Dr. Matheson is an eccentric old pumpkin, I prefer the low-pressure state of my job."

"That's your problem, Lucia. You put all your ambitions and talents into singles bars."

Lucia didn't even flinch—they'd had this argument far too many times for her to take offense. "There's a happy medium, you know. One doesn't have to be always on the lookout as I am. One can just be wise enough not to pass up good opportunities when they come by."

"The first good opportunity, Lucia, and I will

snatch it up quite greedily. I'm just prepared to wait."

"Boring!" Lucia cried. "Let's talk about something more interesting than your nonexistent love life. What are you wearing to the Feinham Gallery opening on Friday?"

"That's four days away—how should I know? I may not even go." Molly yawned extravagantly.

"You know perfectly well you'll go. Jeremy would kill you if you missed his first major opening. Which of your little gentlemen will have the honor of escorting you?"

Molly shrugged. "Probably Julian."

"I wouldn't if I were you. I think Julian's in love with you," Lucia warned, swinging one slender foot idly.

"He only thinks he is because his wife left him and he's lonely. As soon as the situation with Melanie is settled, he'll feel better. Either they'll get back together or he'll look for someone who'll give him more than I'm willing to. In the meantime he's a very pleasant companion."

"Not to mention good-looking."

Molly smiled. "I never said I didn't like to look. I just prefer to keep them at a distance."

With her usual languid grace Lucia rose to her full modellike height of five feet eleven. "I give up on you."

"Thank God for that."

"I'll leave you to your poison-pen letter. Give James Elliott my fond regards."

"I'll do that," Molly replied absently, her mind already on the perfectly polite phrasing of this particular

missive as her hand blindly groped beneath her papers
for another chocolate. She barely noticed Lucia's de-
parture as she contemplated how she could manage to
plant a few veiled insults without being too blatant.
Finding a blank sheet of paper, she fed it into her
Selectric typewriter, rubbing her hands with glee and
chuckling with wicked delight. She'd get her revenge
with words, her most potent weapon, and the elegant
James Elliott would probably not even notice he'd
been cut to ribbons by a master.

"My dear robber baron..." No, that wouldn't
really do for an opening. But she could start her first
draft in such a manner, just to put her in a proper
mood. And then, once started, she couldn't resist.
With wicked delight she called him every name she
could think of, casting aspersions on his family, his
intelligence, his morality, his masculinity, his expertise, and his sanity. The results pleased her enor-
mously, and it was with far better humor that she
began the second draft, studiously polite, with a
gently aggrieved tone that should provoke just the
right amount of remorse in his flintlike heart.

Perfection, she thought, pulling the second sheet
from the typewriter and adding it to the mountain of
paperwork on her desk. It was lucky she served as her
own excellent typist. If she took advantage of the
overworked secretary she shared with three other
people, she'd never have had the pleasure of tearing
Mr. James Elliott apart with such delicious vitupera-
tion. Reaching for a final chocolate, she stared meditatively at the Wyeth painting, musing on the delightful
prospect of that elegant, arrogant man receiving the

first letter. It was a real tragedy that it could never happen. Molly knew better than to let her irritation and doubtful sense of humor get the better of her. Much as she'd like to tell him what a conscienceless creep he was, discretion reared its ugly head. Sighing, she took the neatly typed letter, signed it with a flourish, and tucked it into the pretyped envelope. She never bothered to proofread, and this time was no exception. Shoving the other letter under the pile of paper that littered her desk, she tossed the sealed letter into the out box, leaned back, and contemplated her life.

Chapter Two

"Are you ever going to clean off your desk, Miss McDonough?" No one but the austere Dr. Matheson was allowed to go by his title at the Museum of American Arts, and he blithely disregarded Molly's hard-earned doctorate. "And aren't you slightly over-dressed for work? I realize it's after seven on a Friday evening, but I would think a full-length dress of that silky stuff in that particularly vivid color—"

"It's called seafoam, and I thought it quite subtle," Molly replied, unmoved by her boss's querulousness.

"It makes your eyes look turquoise," Matheson said flatly.

"Thank you."

"It wasn't meant as a compliment. You have perfectly nice blue eyes. Why do you want them to look another color?"

Molly sighed. "Did you want me for anything, sir?"

Dr. Matheson's pale nearsighted eyes peered at her from beneath bushy white eyebrows. "Why are you dressed like that? Are we having another one of these damn cocktail parties?"

"No, sir. Jeremy Cabello's exhibit is opening at the Feinham Gallery. Julian Benson is taking me."

"Benson, eh? Isn't he married?"

"Separated, sir. And we're just friends."

"I've heard that before," the old man snorted, fumbling in his saggy coat pocket for heaven knew what. Molly watched him with fond cynicism. Dr. Henry Matheson's brilliance and acuity in the art world were only matched by his affectations. For the last few months he had been on a binge of senility. He fancied himself a vague old man, and now and then he wandered around, pretending to forget everything that inconvenienced him, becoming marvelously lucid when confronted with a trustee of the museum or a piece of art to be evaluated. "I don't like Cabello's work," he announced abruptly.

"Well, he's not for everyone," Molly agreed.

"So don't be thinking of acquiring anything for us. Our modern wing is overcrowded as it is. And we have to make room for that fellow's new painting." The milky blue eyes were keen beneath the eyebrows, and Molly's senses sharpened. This was why he'd sought her out.

"What fellow's painting?" she questioned carefully, knowing full well what the answer would be.

"Sebastian Coddaire. Used to know the man, didn't you?" He knew as well as anyone that she used to live with him, as he had come to dinner several times at the large untidy loft Molly had shared with the artist.

"I did."

"Well, maybe you can talk him down on his price. It's absurd what he's asking. No living artist ever made as much—at least, not in my day."

"Should he wait until he's dead to make his fortune?" Molly inquired ironically.

"Don't be snippy. The gallery won't bargain, so I want you to put in a word with the fellow. If you can talk him down, there'll be that much more for your folk art collection."

"Sebastian is in Europe, Dr. Matheson," she said patiently, ignoring the carrot he dangled in front of her nose.

"He's due back in the next couple of weeks. I want that painting, Miss McDonough. I'll be counting on you." He turned on his heel with his usual briskness, then remembered his supposed infirmity. With a little skip he turned the briskness into a shuffle, heading out the door, leaving Molly watching him from behind her desk.

Pausing for a moment, he turned back to her, the eyes sharp in the deliberately befuddled face. "Oh, I forgot to mention it. James Elliott called."

Molly was genuinely mystified. "What did he want?"

"To talk to you. Something about a letter."

Feverishly Molly cast her mind back over the unexceptional tone of her second letter. The very slight digs were scarcely enough for him to make a fuss over. "And what did you say?" Her voice came out somewhat dry and raspy, and she cleared her throat.

"I told him you were busy. I wasn't about to give him the time of day." He shuffled off, muttering imprecations about the long-lost pewter platter, leaving

Molly sitting there with an uncharacteristic case of nerves. It was there that Julian Benson found her.

They made a lovely pair, Molly thought cynically, rousing herself from her abstraction. Julian was quite breathtakingly beautiful, with golden hair, longer eyelashes than any man had a right to, and a tall, fit, tanned body that owed its condition to slavish devotion to the tennis courts. It was tennis that had driven his wife, Melanie, away, and Molly couldn't really blame her. Julian was talented in his field, which was banking, but a crashing bore otherwise, particularly when he chose to relive his last few sets.

She gave him her sweetest smile, knowing that the clinging lines of the seafoam dress accentuated her finer points: her high, firm breasts; her small waist; and her lush round hips. It was a sensual dress, bought and worn for her own pleasure, rather than a come-on. She knew she had Julian firmly in line when she had chosen to wear it, but the sudden warmth in his usually chilly blue eyes made her think again.

"You look absolutely marvelous, Lindsay," he said, giving her a lingering kiss on her proffered cheekbone. "I wish we didn't have to go out tonight. Why don't we skip the opening and have dinner down on the Wharf, then go back to your place? I'm sick of all this socializing."

"If we were planning on having dinner at the Wharf and ending up at my apartment, I'd be wearing old jeans, and you wouldn't want to have anything to do with me. Admit it, Julian, you're a very fastidious man." Her voice was lightly mocking, and Julian squirmed just slightly.

"You would always please the most fastidious tastes," he replied in a somewhat strangled attempt at smoothness, and Molly bit back a smile. Puncturing his smoothness kept the romance from his soul, and that was just what she had in mind.

"Bless you, Julian," she murmured. "I can always count on you to say exactly the right thing." She ignored the small wince that marred his handsome tanned face as she reached for the thin silk shawl. "And you'll love Jeremy's paintings—he's really quite talented. And to pay you back for putting up with still another opening, I'll take you to dinner."

The squirm was no longer hidden. "Don't be absurd. I'll pay for dinner." He had to hurry to keep up with her as she glided magnificently down the deserted halls of the administrative section of the museum.

"Don't *you* be absurd," she shot back with typical serenity that would not be denied. "I asked you to accompany me, I'll pay for dinner, or I'll abandon you at the Feinham, at the mercy of all those eccentric artistic types that make you so uncomfortable, and then you'll be sorry." Her smile in no way mitigated the seriousness of her threat.

Julian was still spluttering helplessly as he followed her out of the building into the cool night air. His arguments continued as they drove the few short blocks to the Feinham Gallery, and with accustomed ease Molly tuned him out. What in the world could James Elliott have wanted with her? The letter had been scrupulously polite, merely mentioning the possible fault in ethics of outbidding a curator who'd dis-

covered a particular piece. His ego couldn't be so fragile that even a plaintive question could offend him,
could it? She dearly hoped not. From that brief
glimpse across the gallery she'd been aware of a curious pull. Those eyes, and the austere, almost forbidding expression on his narrow clever face had un-
nerved her, sent her racing out into the night rather
than over to claim an introduction in her usual calm,
self-assured way. She had managed to avoid him since
then, and please God, she'd continue to do so. She
had the melancholy feeling that Julian would provide
no help at all against James Elliott's overpowering
magnetism.

The Feinham Gallery was a bustling, brightly lit, ruthlessly elegant hive of activity. Anyone who had any
claim to distinction in the Bay Area art world, and
many who did not, thronged the richly carpeted
spaces to stare out of slightly alcohol-glazed eyes at
Jeremy Cabello's acrylic and oil visions of the modern
world. Not terribly pleasant, Molly had to admit,
sipping her champagne as she stood elbow to elbow
with an elegant matron in puce silk. Jeremy was abstract and illogical in the extreme, while Molly preferred a more ordered way of life if she couldn't have
raw emotion. Obviously Barry Feinham agreed. The
champagne was a mediocre California vintage. No
Moët for Jeremy, as there had been for Sebastian
Coddaire's first sensational opening.
    Of course, you could never accuse Sebastian of ex-
cessive logic, although he could be at turns puzzlingly
abstract and wickedly realistic. All the life and passion

and vitality seemed to burst forth from his canvases, and Molly had taken one look that night over four years ago and fallen in love. She had fallen in love with his sheer, awesome talent, and then, half an hour later, with his giant's body: six and a half feet of it, with massive shoulders, a shaggy head, and sweet, soulful eyes. And it had taken her two years to realize that all his passion, love, and caring were reserved for his art, and all she was left with was a handsome shell of a man, housing a spoiled, not very interesting little boy. No one had ever since accused her of not being a fast learner.

She gave herself a tiny shake, her curtain of blond hair swinging against her bare shoulders. Why in the world should she get sentimental and nostalgic tonight of all nights? Jeremy's morbid paintings were an unlikely inducement to retrospection. However, there was something about the evening that made her extremely uncomfortable, and she couldn't tell if it was her imagination or some presentiment of disaster.

From the moment she walked in on Julian's arm she had felt ill at ease, as if a thousand eyes were watching her. Julian had abandoned her a few moments after they arrived, cornering a nubile young creature with an available look in her eyes and proceeding to forget Molly entirely.

Not that she minded particularly. She knew more than two thirds of the people there, and she was greeted with warmth and appreciation as she wove her way through the crowds to be one of the few actually there to look at the paintings. And still that strange, uncomfortable feeling of being watched persisted.

This is ridiculous, she told herself sternly after her third furtive glance over her shoulder. *I've never been paranoid before—what's come over me?* Exchanging an empty champagne glass for a full one, she edged away from the crowds, toward the back of the gallery. Barry still had a few works from other artists in the large, poorly lit back room. Last she heard, Sebastian's rendition of the Oregon coast was still in residence. She had always liked his landscapes, she decided fairly, slipping into a deserted hallway and heading toward the back room. And his angry, passionate style would blend well with the Oregon coastline. They had gone there together several times, and she had left him there. How fitting it would be, she decided as she moved into the shadowy room, heading directly for the large painting that dominated the deserted space, to gaze upon the ending of their affair at the scene of its inception.

As usual, Sebastian had outdone himself, and unaccountably Molly felt herself moved to tears. She could feel the angry salt spray on her skin, smell the tang of the sea air—and feel those eyes once again boring into her back. She was no longer alone in the room. Her nemesis had followed her. With a mingled sigh of exasperation and pleasure she turned to meet the expected face of Sebastian Coddaire.

It was therefore a great shock to her that instead of Sebastian's giantlike proportions the man in front of her had a lean, narrow body with a whipcord strength about it. He was tall, perhaps a bit over six feet, but nowhere near Sebastian's mammoth height. His hair was silky black, straight, and cut a trifle long compared to Sebastian's shaggy red mane. His cheekbones were high, his eyebrows winged in his dark, slightly mocking face, his mouth a thin, sensuous line. He was all aristocratic arrogance, from the widow's peak in his raven hair to his expensive leather shoes. Only his eyes didn't quite match. They were a light, almost translucent gray in his dark face, and they looked down at her now with a cold, cynical disdain.

"Have you finished staring at me?" His voice was cool and remote, and belatedly Molly pulled her eyes away, flushing.

"Excuse me, I—I was expecting someone else." Why the hell was she stammering? she thought furiously. And who was this man to stand there like he was god or something? He was staring just as hard at her.

But she already knew exactly who he was—none other than James Elliott. She could at least be grateful to a capricious fate for one thing—he could have no idea who she was.

"I suppose you expected me to be your loutish ex-lover," he said calmly, destroying that fond illusion. It came as no surprise that a stranger would know about her attachment to Sebastian; the Bay Area art world was a very small place when it came to gossip. "I believe he's still in Spain, and will be till the end of the month. I do hope you're not thinking of getting involved with him again. He's a great artist but a fairly wretched human being."

"What the hell business is it of yours?" she demanded hotly, rage temporarily banishing all other emotions.

Thrusting his long, slim hands into the trouser pockets of his elegant black suit, he leaned against the wall next to Sebastian's painting. His studied casual air didn't fool Molly for a moment; he was, if possible, even more tense than she was. There was great anger in the taut set of those shoulders, and the tiny muscle that worked in his cheek was a dead giveaway. His voice, however, was smooth and courteous, and a less observant person would undoubtedly never have noticed the telltale signs of rage.

"Oh, none of my business at all, Ms. McDonough. I would just hate to see someone with such exquisite artistic taste be so indiscriminate in her personal preferences."

His subtle attack threw her off-balance for a moment, but she rallied gamely. Here was the enemy, and he had the gall to bring up the very subject that stood between them. "Yes, I noticed your obvious approval of my taste, Mr. Elliott," she replied in silken tones. "I could only have wished your approval had extended further. It's not very polite," she continued sweetly in what she knew was her most cutting voice, "to wait for some hard-working museum employee to search out valuable acquisitions, do all the research and verifications, and then have you saunter in with an open checkbook and snatch it from under her nose." *There,* she thought with satisfaction. *That should put him in his place.*

James Elliott, however, appeared completely unmoved by her censure. He shrugged carelessly. "But what can you expect from a robber baron?"

The words hit Molly like a blow to the stomach, and

her face paled. "Robber—baron?" she croaked. Damn, there she went stammering again, though this time with good reason.

"Actually, that term better applies to Mr. Seaquist than his humble employee. Of course, I realize you weren't perhaps in the best frame of mind when you sent that letter."

"What letter?" She stalled, knowing it was hopeless. God, how could she have been so stupid, so damnably careless?

He pulled away from the wall, coming to stand in front of her with a curious pantherlike grace. The simile was accurate—he was a feral mountain cat stalking its prey. As he stood over her the large deserted room suddenly seemed small and crowded. She could feel the heat emanating from his body, smell the faint traces of his woodsy after-shave and the lingering scent of pipe tobacco. She looked up at him, boldly, defiantly, and the polite, sneering mask dropped from his dark face, leaving nothing but an awesome fury.

"You know perfectly well what letter, Ms McDonough. That vitriolic little note signed with the ambiguous name of M. L. McDonough. I was getting ready to beat you to a pulp when I realized just who you were." He still looked ready to murder her, and Molly decided to apologize as gracefully as she could.

"Look, that letter was sent by accident," she said hurriedly, backing away from him and coming up against Sebastian's painting. "It was a joke...a way to relieve some frustrations. It was never meant to reach you."

"I can imagine you have some frustrations to relieve," he drawled offensively, those light gray eyes sweeping over her figure.

Molly opened her mouth to let him have it, then closed it again, counting to ten. He had every right to be angry, she admitted fairly. "I'm sorry."

The smile that curved his mouth was anything but pleasant. "I'm sure you are."

Once more her quick temper got the better of her. "But you have to admit I had some provocation. It's absolutely infuriating to—"

"I admit nothing. I had a reason for seeking you out, M. L. McDonough: to explain a few facts of life to your obviously enfeebled brain. For one thing, though I have been called a bastard many times by many people, I am not, in fact, illegitimate. As anyone can plainly see, I am not stupid, crazy, or ignorant about art. Obviously, I have the good taste to agree with you on your judgments."

"Obviously," she echoed bitterly, wishing there were somewhere she could run to.

"But I decided, M. L. McDonough, to give you a demonstration of some of my finer points. For one thing, I am kindhearted enough not to send a copy of your little billet-doux to Dr. Matheson, though no doubt I ought to."

"I—thank you." Those were some of the hardest words she ever had to utter, and her husky voice came out strained.

"And though I ignored most of the insults you heaped upon my head, for some reason I object strongly to being termed light in the pants. I have an aversion to snippety young ladies doubting my masculinity." He was very angry by now, and Molly flinched as his strong tanned hands reached out and caught her upper arms in a bruising grip. "So I thought I would let you judge for yourself." His voice was light and mocking, his face savage, as he yanked her against his iron-hard body and brought his mouth down on hers.

Molly had never been kissed in anger before. Shock and surprise held her rigid for the first few moments, then outrage took over, and she began to struggle. But it was completely useless. His arm across the low-cut back of her dress was an iron band. No matter how she twisted and turned in his furious embrace, she could move no more than a few inches. His other hand caught her jaw, holding her steady as his tongue invaded her helpless mouth, punishing hers in an angry duel. When he felt her acquiesce, accept its bruising presence, his hand moved down to cup her buttocks, pressing her hips against his.

Yes, she thought grimly, tears of rage and pain filling her large blue eyes at the fury of his embrace, light in the pants he definitely was *not*. Two years of celibacy weren't enough to wipe out her memory, and James Elliott felt like a lot more man than she had ever encountered.

Abruptly his mouth pulled away from hers, his pale gray eyes blazing down into her defiant ones. His arms still held her captive against his formidable body, and Molly took a deep, angry breath.

"Get your damn hands off me," she hissed, murder in her face. Slowly, arrogantly, he complied, his arms releasing her trembling body, taking a step back from her with a studied nonchalance belied by his labored breathing.

"That's better," she said. And then she once more closed the distance between their two bodies. Reaching up, she twined her long arms around his neck, pulled his head down, and kissed him full on the mouth, using every ounce of remembered expertise and long-suppressed sensuality she possessed. His mouth opened readily enough to her questing tongue, and all the earlier savagery was banished as she lightly, sweetly, explored his mouth, pressing her full, untrammeled breasts up against his chest. She heard a low groan from the back of his throat, one she unconsciously echoed before pulling out of the too-welcoming circle of his arms.

She grinned up at him. "See ya." And then, turning her back on him, she strolled out of the room, a deliciously satisfied smirk on her face.

She would have been less pleased if she could have seen his expression. James Elliott watched Molly's beautiful, partially-covered back disappear from view with an extremely thoughtful expression in his pale gray eyes, a reluctant grin on his thoroughly kissed mouth. "Well, well," he said gently.

Chapter Three

"So tell me everything you know about James Elliott," Molly demanded as she handed Lucia a cup of espresso. The cup was antique Limoges, covered with pale pink flowers, the table she placed hers on was eighteenth-century English, and the couch she flopped down on was twentieth-century American, Molly having discovered that antique furniture, though possessed of beautiful lines, lacked a great deal in comfort.

She looked around her apartment with pride and satisfaction as Lucia pondered her words. Molly's taste, though excellent, could only be called eclectic, and her apartment showcased it. She lived in an old building, designed by Julia Morgan, the innovative architect who designed part of San Simeon, the estate of J. E. Seaquist's predecessor art collector, William Randolph Hearst. The walls were painted white, the woodwork stripped oak, and each perfect piece of Molly's slowly acquired collection of treasures glowed, from the pie safe with its pierced-tin panels, which Molly guiltily recognized belonged in a museum, to the muted tones of the Carolina lily quilt that graced the wall over the pale blue sofa; from the display of nineteenth-century game boards and basketry, to the vibrant, passionate colors of Sebastian's parting gift to her, a brilliantly tender mother and child that would have put Mary Cassatt to shame.

She had had her work cut out for her, prying that one painting from Sebastian's greedy clutches. He valued his work, and the extraordinary amounts of money it brought in, and it was only when he realized that Molly might very well leave him that he reluctantly parted with one. Molly could never understand why she had chosen such a tender, maternal scene. She would have been far wiser to have chosen something less sentimental, which in the long run would have been of more intrinsic value. Or, if she really had had her own welfare in mind, she would have chosen the two flamboyant nudes he had done of her. Sebastian had termed them dreadful smears but refused to acquiesce to her demands to either destroy them or give them up to her. So somewhere in Sebastian's storage were two embarrassingly intimate oils of Mary Lindsay McDonough, shamelessly nude and staring out at the world, sensuously yet defiantly. It was that sensuality Sebastian had wanted to capture, but the defiance had crept out, in the thrust of one creamy hip, and in the curve of her full breasts. He had tried again, with the same results and the added problem of Molly catching the flu from lying nude in his drafty loft, and then he'd given up, telling her she was useless as a model. But Molly always had the suspicion that it hadn't been her failure as a model, or his dissatisfaction with his own artistic product, that had put him in such a temper, but that he hadn't been able to make her what he wanted her to be. The defiance had always come through, and his artistic honesty hadn't let him ignore it.

"James Elliott," Lucia said meditatively, breaking Molly's reverie. "I don't think anyone knows much about him. I gather he went to one of those eastern universities—Princeton, I think. Word has it he was married and divorced long ago, and that his connection with Seaquist is long-standing. His particular field of expertise is— I don't think you're going to like this, Lindsay."

Molly took a sip of her cooling coffee. "I can imagine."

"American decorative and folk art, I'm afraid, just like you. He also knows a great deal about modern American painting, and is generally pretty knowledgeable in most other areas."

Molly shifted restlessly, remembering the look in his eyes as he caught sight of Sebastian's *Oregon Coastline*. "I'm sure he is. Do you suppose he's after Matheson's job? Sounds like he's cut out to be head of a museum with his general knowledge."

"I think he's going to stay on with Seaquist. Something's going on with the old man. I can't believe he'd suddenly have Hearst-like ambitions after a long, fairly respectable life."

"You can never tell. He might have got senile. He's such a determined hermit, he must have at least a streak of Howard Hughes in him. I bet he fancies himself an Egyptian pharaoh, and he's hired Elliott to amass all the art of the western world to be entombed with him.''

"What a gruesome thought, Lindsay! You have the strangest imagination sometimes. Do you suppose he'll have his wives and servants entombed with him?"

"Let's just hope Elliott's among them," Molly snapped.

"Oh, I don't know." Lucia stretched out her long slim legs. "He sounds rather dreamy to me. I wish every man that got mad at me would kiss me."

"It wasn't the pleasant experience you fancy, Lucia," Molly said dryly.

"So why did you kiss him back?"

"To teach him a lesson!"

"And is that all? Are you certain you didn't enjoy having a warm male body pressed up against you for a change?" She tossed her curly mane of chestnut hair, eyeing Molly through knowing brown eyes.

Molly opened her mouth to deny it, then closed it again. "It *was* a nice body," she admitted ruefully.

"I knew it!" Lucia crowed. "Now we have to figure out what our next step is. You can't let go of such a promising beginning."

"I most certainly can. I don't want—" The telephone's sharp ring broke into her hot denials, and she picked it up, snapping unnecessarily.

The agitated squawking forced her to hold the phone several inches from her ear, and it was moments before she recognized Dr. Matheson's usually cultured tones beneath the hysteria.

"He's done it!" the voice shrieked. "He actually had the nerve to do it! He may think I'm a senile old fool, unable to defend myself against his robbing and pillaging, but he'll have another think coming. I'm not ready to be counted out yet, not by any means. I'll have that SOB sorry he ever tried to tamper with Henry Matheson! I'll—"

"Who? Who's done what to you, Dr. Matheson? Has something happened to the museum?"

"Of course something's happened to the museum, you ninny! Do you think anything else could upset me so? It's that bastard Elliott."

"James Elliott?" Molly asked frankly, and Lucia's eyebrows rose across the room. "What's he done now?"

"I'll tell you what he's done! He's stolen Coddaire's painting from me—*Oregon Coastline*—that's what he's stolen. He went to Barry Feinham last night and offered him full price for it. And Barry, damn his soul, took it."

"Well, you *were* trying to hold out for a lower price," Molly said faintly. "You can't blame him if someone is willing to pay full price."

"Whose side are you on? I certainly can blame him. Feinham knew I wanted that painting, knew I'd pay full price if I had to. And he didn't even have the courtesy to let me make a counteroffer."

"He probably thought you wouldn't be willing to go any higher, since you were reluctant to pay the full price in the first place."

"He had no right to make that assumption. I hardly think I'm being unreasonable if I feel that twenty thousand dollars is a bit steep for a painting by a living artist.''

"Twenty thousand—" Molly gasped, her eyes straying to the graceful mother and child on her wall.

"That's what he's getting for some of his larger paintings," Matheson fretted.

"Well, in that case I think we're better off without it," she said, not without a pang. She had been taken with the painting the moment she set eyes on it last night, and the thought of Elliott snatching it from under their noses was anathema to her.

"We're not going to do without it, McDonough!" Matheson said sternly. "You're going to get it back."

"I am?" Molly squawked. "How could I possibly do that?"

"You know Barry Feinham quite well, don't you? He wasn't about to give me Elliott's home phone number and address, and this can't wait until Monday, when he may or may not show up at his office. I want you to call Feinham, sweet-talk him into giving you Elliott's phone number, and—"

"And then you'll call Elliott?" she supplied hopefully.

"Certainly not. *You* will phone him. I gather the two of you disappeared for half an hour last night. You must be pretty well acquainted by now. As a matter of fact, if you already know where he is—"

"I do not! And we did not disappear. He happened to follow me into Barry's back room—" The moment the words were out of her mouth she could have bitten her tongue.

Matheson had long since discarded his senile act.

"He followed you into the back room!" His tones held awesome rage. "And that's where he saw the painting?"

"I'm afraid so," Molly admitted, wishing there were some way out of it.

"Then I hold you directly responsible, and you had better do your damnedest to remedy the situation. You have Feinham's number—I'll expect a full report from you on Monday morning." The phone slammed down, and Molly stared at her receiver in consternation.

"Sounds like Matheson's on the warpath again," Lucia said sympathetically. "Why has he picked you to be his victim?"

"Because of James Damn-him Elliott. He's bought that painting of Sebastian's that Matheson was so hot for, and Matheson wants me to get it back."

"So you have to beard the lion in his den? I guess that answers my question."

"What question?" Molly said absently, searching through her blue tooled-leather address book for the phone number of the Feinham Gallery. The sooner she got this over with the better.

"What your next step is going to be with James Elliott. It appears that Dr. Matheson has already figured that out. Somehow I can't imagine the old man as cupid," Lucia mused.

"Don't be absurd, Lucia. This is business," Molly said repressively, her cheeks flushed, her blue eyes sparkling, the right dimple very much in evidence as she dialed Barry Feinham's number.

"Dr. Matheson's been screaming at me," she said

in reply to Barry's friendly inquiry. "He wants me to wrest Sebastian's Oregon painting from James Elliott with my bare hands. I presume he already tried to offer you more money?"

"He did, M. L., and it broke my heart to refuse him. There's nothing I would have liked more than to have got higher than asking price from the old skin-flint. But I've given my word to Elliott—there's not a thing I can do at this point."

"No, I suppose not. I'll have to deal with him myself. Could you give me his home address and phone number?"

There was a long pause. "I don't see how I could do that, M. L., much as I'd like to oblige. It's a question of client privacy, after all.... Hold on a minute, will you, M. L.?" She could hear a short, muffled conversation in the background, and then Barry's sculptured New York tones came back on the line. "His phone is unlisted, M. L. Sorry. But his address is forty-one seventy-one Kensington. He has the upper two floors, I think."

"Uh...thanks, Barry. I appreciate your breach of etiquette." And distrusted it strongly, she added silently.

"No problem, M. L. Just don't forget you owe me one."

"I won't forget," she promised, wondering if it was revenge or gratitude she owed him.

"So you're going to see him? On his home turf and everything?" Lucia queried.

Molly shrugged with a fine attempt at unconcern that fooled neither of them. "I guess I don't have any choice in the matter," she said negligently, and then her mouth broke into a wide grin. "Come and help me pick out what to wear."

Lucia's eyes lit up. "So you've decided to go for him?" she demanded as she followed her into the bedroom.

"Certainly not," Molly replied saucily. "I just want him to appreciate what he's missing."

"Wretch!" Lucia said feelingly. "I could almost feel sorry for the poor man."

"So could I," she agreed. "Almost, but not quite."

Chapter Four

Not even Lucia could find fault with Molly's attire as she made her way across town to the semiresidential section that housed James Elliott. Businesslike but casual, the two of them had decreed, and she was now attired in a turquoise silk blouse, unbuttoned a discreet two buttons to hint at the deep cleft between her breasts, and beige linen pants that showed off her long legs and disguised her full hips. Her blond hair was brushed into a shining sweep and left hanging loose, and she carried a suede jacket over her shoulder against the chilling autumn afternoon. Nothing betrayed the rapid beating of her heart or her damp palms, but the shining, excited eyes were a dead giveaway. She could only hope her new nemesis wasn't observant. She knew it to be a vain hope.

4171 Kensington came as a surprise to Molly. She would have expected James Elliott to live in a penthouse, surrounded by glass and steel, protected from the real world, head in the clouds. Instead, he had chosen an apartment in one of the renovated old town houses of San Francisco, this one painted a warm dusky rose. Her hand trailed along the pale oak hand-rail as she climbed the two flights of stairs to Elliott's duplex. There was no flashy car outside—he'd definitely drive a Jaguar or a Mercedes—so maybe he wasn't home. She could knock on his door, leave her card with her phone number, and escape back across town, to the safety of her apartment.

Now, why did she think of it in those terms? she wondered, pausing outside the massive door with its discreet brass plate. Escape and safety—surely James Elliott wasn't that much of a threat to her? Only if she allowed him to be.

She turned the old-fashioned doorbell, hoping there would be no answer. For a blessed few moments she thought her prayers would be answered, and then came the unmistakable sounds of someone dealing with the lock. For a moment she was tempted to turn and race down the stairs before that solid oak door opened. But there was a peephole—Elliott would have seen her and would doubtless be greatly amused to catch her running from him like the coward she was. Resolutely she stood her ground.

The door swung open, and she immediately regretted her decision. He was even more devastating than she remembered. He was leaning against the door-jamb, his shirt sleeves rolled up to reveal tanned, muscled forearms that tapered into long beautiful hands. His thick black hair was rumpled, as if he'd been taking a nap, his pale gray eyes surveyed her with cool amusement, and that thin sensuous mouth smiled at her with only a trace of mockery.

"I expected you earlier," he drawled without any

preamble. "What have you been doing all afternoon?" He moved aside to let her in, but only a small amount. Molly hesitated, and then strode boldly ahead, determined not to let him intimidate her. Her arm brushed against him, and it was all she could do not to jerk away. She continued calmly ahead, determined to ignore the strong physical effect the man had on her.

Just as sternly she forced herself to ignore the very intense aesthetic pleasure the apartment gave her. Most of the interior walls had been knocked out, leaving one huge white plastered room. The old mahogany floors had been stripped and polished and each piece of furniture and artwork had been carefully chosen. She couldn't recognize any particular piece. Apparently, all his pilfered acquisitions really did go to some giant vault belonging to J. E. Seaquist.

"You were expecting me?" she queried calmly, turning to face him as he shut the door with a quiet, well-oiled click.

"I was. Would you like some coffee? Or a drink? It's after five already." He headed toward the open kitchen area of the large room with his peculiarly sinuous grace. "Or how about Irish coffee? It's a raw day."

"That would be very nice. I suppose you were in Barry's office when I called." It was a stab in the dark, and he smiled in sardonic amusement as he busied himself with the coffee.

"Right the first time," he acknowledged. "We had just closed the deal."

"Then why did you let him give me your address?

And why didn't you have him give me your so-called unlisted number?'' She kept the indignation out of her voice with a strong effort, casting her eye about her for a suitable place to sit. An old three-sided eighteenth-century bed had been turned into a sofa, the thick natural cotton upholstery and pillows being just the sort of thing to curl up against. Molly eyed it longingly, taking a small upright chair that was alarmingly uncomfortable.

You never struck me as obtuse, M. L. McDonough,'' he replied.

"I'm not usually so. You wanted me to come here."

"Of course."

"But why? You aren't thinking of changing your mind about Sebastian's painting, are you?'' She sat warily, on the edge of her chair, as he deftly whipped some cream with a wire whisk. She had never been able to manage that feat without an electric beater, and she eyed him with a mixture of distrust and admiration.

"I'm not about to change my mind about Coddaire's painting. It's one of the best things he's ever done, and it will go admirably with the other works in the Seaquist collection. He doesn't have nearly enough moderns."

"Thank heavens for that. Maybe you'll filch acquisitions from someone else for a change."

"You know there's nothing really unethical or immoral about what I've been doing,'' he remarked from across the room.

"I disagree. Apart from any ethical considerations

in the way you go about finding certain pieces, I happen to consider it immoral to have works of art hidden away from the public, hoarded like some obscene treasure for a demented old miser to play with."

She could tell by the tightening of his jaw that she had angered him, just as she had hoped to. "Seaquist is not a demented old miser," he corrected her icily. "And *I* happen to think that art should be used and enjoyed by people, not hung away in museums where no one can touch or feel it. Art should be lived with."

"If you had your way, a great many irreplaceable masterpieces would be destroyed," she snapped.

"And if I were an artist, I'd rather have my work destroyed than put in a soul-crushing institution like a museum," he snarled right back. And then his temper vanished, leaving a rueful smile curving that sensual mouth. "I promised myself I wasn't going to fight with you, M. L. McDonough." He came toward her, carrying the Irish coffee. The smell was heavenly, and he'd been more than generous with the whipped cream. Molly's stomach did a little leap of anticipation.

Walking right by her, he went to sit on the sofa bed, leaning against the pile of cushions and smiling at her sweetly. "If you want your coffee, you have to come and get it."

"I don't think there's any reason for me to stay," she said coolly, rising to her full five feet six inches, wishing desperately for Lucia's majestic height. It was difficult to be regal at five feet six. "If you have no intention of changing your mind about Sebastian's painting—"

"I wouldn't have thought you'd give in so easily," he chided gently. "Are you afraid of me?"

"Certainly not!" she snapped.

"Then come over here and have your coffee," he drawled. "I promise I won't bite. You haven't even tried to change my mind yet."

She hesitated for only a moment. Leaving might be the wisest course, but she hated to appear a coward in front of him. She hadn't let any man get the better of her in years, including Sebastian, and she had no desire to start with James Elliott. "All right," she agreed, crossing the polished expanse of flooring and taking a seat beside him on the sofa bed, as far away from his long, lean body as she could. "How can I make you change your mind?"

A slow, suggestive smile lit his face, and her temper snapped. "Must you relate everything to the bedroom? If you think I'm going to sleep with you in return for Sebastian's painting, you must be out of your mind."

"And you must have delusions of grandeur. You're quite luscious, but I wouldn't have thought you'd be worth twenty thousand dollars," he said solemnly, a light in his eyes betraying his amusement.

"You'll never know," she said loftily, sipping her coffee, her tongue snaking out to capture the line of whipped cream that frosted her upper lip.

"And why won't I?" he questioned, his eyes on her mouth. "Who's to say we won't fall madly in love and have an intense, passionate affair?"

She ignored the little thrill of excitement that ran

down her spine at the thought. "I say so. My life is very comfortable as it is."

"Well, then, who's to say we won't have a passionate one-night stand?" he countered.

"I happen to be enjoying the new celibacy, Mr. Elliott. I have no need or interest in any kind of relationship right now, either long-term or short," she said loftily. She was unprepared for his burst of laughter.

"Well, that explains the tame eunuchs you've been running around with the last few months," he said when his mirth had subsided a bit. "And my name is James. Don't you think, after all we've shared, that we ought to be on a first-name basis?"

"Certainly, James," she said with false sweetness. "I do hope you're enjoying yourself at my expense. There's nothing I like better than to provide amusement to bored dilettantes."

It should have cut him to the quick. Instead, he laughed again. "You think I'm a bored dilettante?"

"At best," she snapped.

"My dear M. L. McDonough, you are priceless," he said, leaning back against the pillows and watching her out of smiling eyes. "But I still don't like that name. What do your friends call you? What does M. L. stand for?"

"My friends call me M. L.," she said frostily. She should get up and leave, she knew perfectly well she should, but James Elliott was having a mesmerizing effect on her. She wanted to stay, sitting beside him on this far-too-comfortable sofa bed, and try to cut

him down to size. He seemed to be firmly possessed
of the upper hand, but Molly wasn't about to give in.
"You hardly qualify as such, so why don't you settle
on Ms McDonough? Or, even better, Dr. McDonough."

"You may as well tell me what the initials stand
for," he continued, unperturbed by her suggestions,
his long beautiful fingers playing with the thin Water-
ford crystal of her Irish coffee goblet. "I'll find out
sooner or later—you may as well give in."

"Mary Lindsay," she muttered, her husky voice
graceless.

"Mary Lindsay," he mused, his eyes playing over
her stiff frame like a caress. "You certainly aren't a
Mary—you're far too earthy and sensuous for that. I
don't see any pure, madonnalike tendencies about
you. And Lindsay is too masculine. A Lindsay should
be a lean, tawny beast, not a soft, round, feminine
little creature like you. I think I'll call you Molly."
One hand reached out and gently pulled her hair away
from her face. "Like Molly Bloom—a lustful Irish
wench."

"You certainly won't call me Molly! That's my
father's name for me." She should have slapped his
hand away, but her own hands remained clasped
loosely enough in her lap.

The fingers traced her delicate jawline. "I don't
think you'll get the two of us confused," he drawled,
and the feel of his hands on her skin was like fire and
ice. He caught her chin firmly, turning her averted
profile to face him. "Do you?"

"Actually, the two of you look somewhat alike.

Perhaps that's why I'm putting up with so much from you—you remind me of Daddy.''

"You wretch!" He released her chin and sat up quickly, a rueful grin on his face. "You certainly are adept at unmanning someone. So you got your glorious blond hair from your mother?"

"I'm adopted," she said shortly. "I have no idea where my blond hair comes from."

He contented himself with one curious look before he bounded off the sofa. "Where do you want to go for dinner?"

It took her a moment to react. "To my apartment. Alone."

"Too bad," he said sympathetically, leaning over her. "If you don't go out to dinner with me, you won't have a snowball's chance in hell of getting Coddaire's painting. And I might also be tempted to send Matheson a copy of your charming little letter."

"That's blackmail!" she gasped, outraged.

He nodded. "I admit to being unscrupulous. Put it down to a detestation of eating alone." He straightened up, stretching casually, and Molly found her eyes wandering over his body like a starving kitten. He was long and lean, far more slender than Sebastian's burly bulk, and yet there was some question in her mind as to who would be the stronger. There was a tightly leashed strength about James's lean body, a quickness and litheness that Sebastian had lacked. She wondered if he was as taut and lean as he appeared to be without his clothes, and whether he was smooth-skinned or covered with fine black hair. She looked up to meet his eyes.

It was a decided shock. She had no doubt whatsoever that he knew exactly what had been running through her mind as her eyes took inventory of his body, but he said nothing, contenting himself with a faint smile. "Where do you want to eat?"

She hesitated for a moment longer. "Someplace with seafood," she said finally, waiting for him to preen with typical male triumph. Once more he caught her off guard, merely nodding casually as he moved away. She watched him with mixed feelings, among them irritation, anticipation, and regret. What the hell was she doing, getting involved with someone like James Elliott? For the first time in two years she had lost control of her life. Someone else had come along and upset the even tenor of it, and no matter how hard she tried, she couldn't put him in his place along with the other—what was his name for them?— tame eunuchs.

She'd take one more stab. "You know who you remind me of?" Her husky voice sounded across the room, and he paused in the act of putting on a beautifully tailored wine corduroy jacket.

"Attila the Hun?" he offered wryly. "Jack the Ripper?"

"Nothing quite so macho," she said sweetly. "No, you remind me of Darcy, in—"

"Yes, I know, *Pride and Prejudice*." Without missing a beat he shrugged into the jacket, crossed the room, and pulled her to her feet, both hands holding her forearms in a light yet possessive clasp. When he looked down at her like that, his gray eyes warm and laughing, it was all she could do to fight the insidious attraction he held for her. "That's unfortunately a bit too accurate. I do have more than my fair share of pride. And you, M. L. McDonough, have too much prejudice. Would you allow that possibility?"

When he looked at her like that, she would allow him almost anything. "It's possible," she said slowly, and smiled back quite shyly, the dimple appearing beside her mouth.

He stared at her for a long moment. "And I think I prefer Molly Bloom to Elizabeth Bennett," he said softly, and he darted down, brushing a light, butterfly kiss against her smiling mouth, pulling away before she could react. "Let's go."

Chapter Five

James had chosen well, Molly thought as she leaned against the soft ancient leather seat of the banquette in their corner booth. Dmitrios's was a picturesquely seedy Greek tavern that made up for its lack of elegance with excellent food and a warm, homelike atmosphere that began at once to ease Molly's strained, suspicious nerves. But, of course, James knew exactly what he was doing—never had she known anyone so completely, frustratingly in control.

Outright hostility amused him, her barbs, intended to demoralize him, bounced right off, and her calculated efforts at condescending charm elicited only a raised eyebrow.

"You may as well not bother," he said halfway through dinner. He'd been either unimaginative or self-assured enough to have chosen moussaka, accompanying it with a slightly woodsy Médoc rather than the traditional retsina.

"Bother?" she echoed innocently between dainty bites of broiled swordfish.

His eyelids drooped mockingly over his light gray

eyes. "That wide-eyed innocence won't do you any good either. You know perfectly well what I'm talking about. You can't make me jump the way you want, so you might as well give up and enjoy yourself."

Stalling for time, she picked up her glass of white wine and took a slow, appreciative sip. With typically masculine high-handedness he'd ordered it for her, and much as she wanted to, she couldn't fault him for his choice. It was crisp and cool and light, perfectly suited to the swordfish. It should have come as no surprise that his taste in wine, as well as in everything else, was faultless.

"And exactly what would giving up entail?" she inquired carefully, images of her suppliant body stretched out at his feet flitting through her mind. It was a place she had a strange desire to be, and she could only attribute the aberration to an excess of wine.

His smile lit his dark face. "Nothing so very terrible," he said soothingly, his voice running over her skin like molten silver. "Just relaxing a bit. I'm not all that dangerous, you know. I won't bite you."

She smiled, her slow, sweet smile that gave him a tantalizing view of the dimple on her right cheek. "Aren't you? Dangerous, I mean. I would think you're very dangerous, indeed. To someone vulnerable to your particular brand of charm, that is."

Only a faint blink showed that her barb had finally hit home this time. "And you're not, of course. Not vulnerable, to me, or to anyone else. Is that the message you've been struggling to give me?"

How had he got so close? When they'd started the

meal there had been a good two feet between them on the banquette. Now he was a bare few inches away, the heat from his thigh burning into hers, his chest seductively close to her face. He was very potent, and well he knew it, but Molly knew she was more than a match for him—or at least, she dearly hoped so.

"If I've been struggling, it's only because you refuse to listen," she said in her enchantingly husky voice. "I have chosen not to be interested in involvements and entanglements at this time in my life, and that makes me invulnerable. Not that you aren't very charming with all your blandishments, but I'm afraid they leave me quite unmoved."

He quirked an eyebrow at her. "Oh, really? I hadn't noticed I was throwing out any lures. I'll do my best to moderate my behavior." His thigh brushed hers so lightly, she would almost have thought it an accident if it weren't for the small pleased smile in those piercing gray eyes. Her irritation didn't keep her from reacting. Much as her instincts told her to press closer, her brain ordered her to retreat, and she did so, to the far edge of the banquette.

"A few more inches and you'll be on the floor, Molly," he observed calmly, leaning back. "And if you're as invulnerable as you claim, I don't understand why you're so skittish."

"I am not skittish!" she snapped, frustration getting the better of her.

"Like a high-strung mare," he added, ignoring her angry disclaimer.

"And you think you're the one to break me to bridle?" she fought back.

His hand reached and brushed her cheek, gently, soothingly, and she flinched away, rather than give in to the almost overwhelming urge to butt her head against that stroking hand like a docile mare rather than the nerve-ridden horse he alluded to. "No, Molly Bloom," he murmured, his voice playing along her nerves like a thousand dancing butterflies. "I wouldn't want to lead you anywhere against your will." A wicked gleam lit his eyes, and the atmosphere suddenly lightened. "If anything, I picture you as a shy young brood mare."

She couldn't help herself. Responding to the humorous glint in his eyes, she found herself laughing. "And I can guess who my chosen stud would be."

He laughed with her, and the sound of their mingled amusement was strangely more intimate than their previous semierotic bantering. "My bloodlines are proven," he agreed with a wicked smile. "Though I don't know if I quite qualify as a stallion. . . ."

Oh, yes, you do, Molly thought, remembering the feel of his angry masculinity pressed up against her at the Feinham Gallery. And then, unbidden, a deep blush stained her cheeks, amusing him even more.

"Maybe we'd better change the subject," he suggested, a hint of laughter still in his deep voice.

"I think that would be a good idea." Molly's voice was muffled, and she carefully kept her face averted from the wicked delight in his. Score another point for him, she thought morosely. No matter how hard she tried, she couldn't seem to throw him off-balance. As a matter of fact, he seemed far more adept at disconcerting *her*.

"Have you suddenly got shy?" His voice teased her gently. "I wouldn't have thought you'd be so delicate."

She forced herself to meet his gaze. "That isn't the word I'd use. I just think discussing your...physical endowments...is a bit intimate after such a brief acquaintance."

His eyes lit up. "Is that what we were discussing?" he marveled. "I thought we were discussing horses."

He was waiting for her to blush again, but this time she had her reactions firmly under control. "Stallions, Mr. Elliott," she corrected.

He let it pass. "I don't know if I'd call it a brief acquaintance. We made a lot of progress in a very short time last night."

There was no reply she could make to that without compromising herself. He rose in one fluid move, looming over her as she kept her eyes on the remains of her swordfish. "I'll let you meditate on that while I go speak with Dmitrios. You can either plan a snotty comeback or choose your dessert—whichever gives you more pleasure." A moment later he was moving across the crowded restaurant with that effortless grace that was an integral part of him. She watched him go with mixed emotions, foremost among them a craving to bring him down to the level of her so-called tame eunuchs. But it was rapidly becoming apparent that James Elliott would never fit into that category.

So far he had steadfastly refused to discuss Sebastian's painting, and Molly had almost forgotten that that was ostensibly the reason she was here with him tonight. It was no wonder, she told herself with her customary honesty. Sebastian's painting was the farthest thing from her mind right now. She was here with James Elliott because she wanted to be. If she hadn't wanted his dangerous company, all his threats and lures would have done him no good at all.

Dispassionately she allowed her eyes to roam over his well-made frame. His jacket and slacks were obviously tailor-made, and they accentuated his lean, firmly-muscled body. Molly let her eyes trail up his long, long legs, the narrow waist, the deceptively lean physique that she had already discovered held a great deal of power. She was not a weak woman herself, but she was no match for James Elliott's wiry strength. His straight black hair brushed the nape of his neck, and Molly knew a sudden, overpowering desire to brush it aside and press her mouth against his vulnerable skin. And then he would turn, pulling her into his arms, holding her tautly against his fiery warmth, and she would say yes.

As if he could read her thoughts, James turned suddenly from his conversation with his old friend Dmitrios, the gentle, friendly owner of the tavern. Those gray eyes darkened to a smoldering depth as they caught the sudden, unbidden longing in her face. There was a promise in those eyes as they burned into Molly's, a promise that warmed and terrified her. The silence of that vibrant, steamy communication lasted for a breathless moment, and then he turned back to Dmitrios, following him into the kitchen in response to a jovial invitation.

When his lean, straight back had disappeared beyond the swinging door, Molly leaned back against the banquette, dazed. She felt as if she'd run several miles. Her heart was pounding, her palms were sweaty, her breathing was rapid, and her knees felt curiously, damnably weak.

How could this have happened? she demanded of herself shakily. After two long, wonderfully invulnerable years, how could an arrogant, ruthless, undeniably handsome man throw her for such a loss? She'd never had much of a weakness for handsome men, preferring character to beauty. Well, James Elliott had character, all right, and more than enough physical beauty besides. And the thought of him returning to sit next to her on the banquette, his thigh pressed up against hers, his devastating eyes stripping her soul bare, made her feel weak with longing and resentment.

With sudden decisiveness Molly grappled around for her purse. They'd driven across town in Molly's white Peugeot; it would be horribly rude of her to leave him stranded. It was bad enough to contemplate running out on him after dinner without a word—to leave him without transportation was unconscionable. She hesitated, her eyes straying to the rough cotton napkin he'd tossed casually by his empty plate. And she remembered the way his beautiful hands had crushed the napkin, remembered how those long dark fingers had reached up to gently stroke the side of her face, the touch of flesh on flesh fiery. If anything would demoralize her, it was those hands.

Thirty seconds later she was gone. Sixty seconds later the Peugeot was in gear racing down the empty streets. Four hundred and eighty seconds later James

Elliott stared out at the deserted street, a slightly grim expression to his mouth, a glint in his eyes.

"Coward," he chided softly to the cool night air. "My point, I believe." And he started back into the tavern for another glass of wine with his old friend Dmitrios, and eventually, to call a taxi.

Chapter Six

The storm broke shortly after ten o'clock on Monday morning. Molly had made it through the remainder of Saturday night and Sunday locked safely away in her apartment. Lucia had gone away for the weekend with one of her latest young men, and Molly's widowed father had been in Oregon, visiting his recently acquired lady friend, a motherly widow with a large, happy brood of children and grandchildren.

Molly had listened to her father's enthusiastic descriptions of their chaotic family life with mixed emotions, part longing for the large, happy family she and her father had always been denied, part jealousy of the new woman in her father's life, part joy for his well-deserved and long-delayed happiness. After her adoptive mother's cool efficiency, Charles McDonough deserved the easygoing warmth of Elinor Hazelton, and Molly was the last to begrudge him his newfound happiness. Sarah McDonough had been dead for three years now, her last, silent, grimly fought battle with cancer over without her having uttered a complaint or a word of regret for her long, lonely life. If she had voiced a regret to the devoted, patient husband and adopted daughter who kept a vigil by her bed those last days, Molly knew too well what it would have been: regret for the children she could never bear; regret that she had adopted a three-week-old baby girl with the mistaken assumption that once the adoption was final she would automatically conceive. Hadn't all her friends assured her that was exactly what would happen? But as her adopted daughter had prospered and grown, no biological children had filled Sarah McDonough's ruthlessly concave belly, and her resentment had spilled over onto Molly's innocent head.

Molly had known from early on that she had failed her mother, that she was there on sufferance. Fortunately, Charles McDonough had more than made up for his wife's lack of maternal warmth, and the bond between the two of them was strong and unshakable. And over the years a mild affection and grudging respect had grown between adoptive mother and daughter. Three years after Sarah's last pain-ridden hours, Molly couldn't begrudge the comfort and warmth her father found with Elinor. She only wished she could find a share of it.

Elinor had always been studiously polite the few times they'd met, her faded blue eyes anxious as she tried to bridge the inevitable gap between herself and her dear friend's daughter. Molly wished she knew how to bridge that gap herself, to tap into the warmth and love Elinor obviously had in abundance and wanted to share. But something, some ancient, ingrained fear of intimacy inherited from the cold-blooded Sarah McDonough, kept Molly at a distance that Elinor sorrowfully respected.

So, on Sunday, assured that no one she had any desire to see was in town, Molly had turned off her telephone and spent the day baking bread, watching old movies on television, and working on the quilt she had started when she thought she would marry Sebastian Coddaire. The engagement had failed, but it was still a very beautiful quilt, of a bridal wreath appliqué that Molly was now busily quilting with tiny, perfect stitches. If she had checked her answering service too many times for an irate, mocking phone call that never came, the fresh bread and butter had served to distract her. With truly remarkable willpower she had banished the feeling of impending doom that hung over her like a storm cloud.

She'd only been at her abysmally messy desk for an hour when she heard Matheson's noisy approach down the hall and knew with a sinking feeling that he was heading in her direction. The senile old man act had been replaced by the irascible eccentric, and Molly wasn't sure which she preferred.

She had had the vague, idealistic hope that James Elliott, touched by her obscure charm, had relented his decision. The daydreams had even gone so far as to envision the huge painting delivered to her personally with a dozen roses and a brief, evocative note saying something delightful, such as "Forgive me?" or "Have dinner with me?" or "Sleep with me?" One look at Matheson's mottled face as he charged into her office was enough to assure her that the only note

Elliott might send her would be one of triumphant self-congratulation.

"Well, you certainly made a fine mess of it this time!" Matheson fumed, slamming the door behind him in a controlled fury and standing in front of her desk, his body bristling with rage. "I thought I could count on you to handle delicate negotiations, but you appear to have handled this particular situation with all the tact of a she-elephant in labor."

"I presume you're talking about James Elliott and Sebastian's picture of the Oregon coast?" she said wearily, rising to her feet with automatic courtesy.

"Sit down," Matheson snapped, following his own order. "And what else would I be talking about? Not only do you lead the man directly to a painting I was negotiating for, you do absolutely nothing to change his mind. I thought you were capable of better things, McDonough."

"But—"

"When I spoke to Feinham this morning, he told me Elliott had the painting shipped on Sunday morning!" he continued, ignoring her faint cry of protest. "He didn't wait for the ink to dry on the check. And do you know what that man said when I called him?"

"Which man?" Molly was getting confused. "Barry?"

"Don't add deliberate obtuseness to your other sins, McDonough," he said harshly. "I wasn't about to let this pass without a formal protest. And Elliott couldn't have been more charming. Said to thank you for bringing that painting to his attention—that it was perfect for the Seaquist collection. And he said to tell you he was looking forward to whatever new pieces you came up with." Matheson slammed a fist down on her desk, and the papers jumped. "What are you going to do about this, McDonough?"

"I don't know," she replied blankly.

"You must have done something to arouse the man's anger. He's out to get you, and with the power of the Seaquist millions behind him, the museum will be powerless to stop him from ruining you."

She found she could agree with him—James Elliott *was* out to get her—but she had the ominous feeling that a shattered career was far from his eventual goal. The look in his pale gray eyes had been much too heated. "I don't really think he's out to ruin me, Dr. Matheson," she said consideringly. "I've made him angry, but I somehow don't think he's the type to hold a grudge, or ruin a career on a whim."

"You can't imagine how gratifying it is to hear you defend the man. You certainly seem to know him quite well for someone who just met him," Matheson observed peevishly. "I don't want you tangling with him again."

"But—"

"If the museum and Elliott both want the same piece in the future, we'll have someone else negotiate it. Jones-Baldwin or Michaels will be a bit more capable of holding their own against a shark like Elliott. You're simply not up to his weight, McDonough."

"That remark sounds ominously sexist, Dr. Matheson," Molly said in a dangerous undertone. She was not Sarah McDonough's daughter for nothing. "Are you suggesting that only a man is capable of dealing with a robber baron like Elliott?" She found herself flinching as the remembered unfortunate words came out of her mouth.

"No," he said, not at all cowed. "Lucia Caldwell would be equally adept at getting what she wanted from the man—using other tactics, of course. Don't worry, McDonough. At some point I'll give you a chance to prove yourself again. You're obviously just a trifle less experienced and astute than you appear. A few more years under your belt, dealing with types like Elliott, and you'll be able to hold your own in this dog-eat-dog world."

It was his condescending dismissal that put the finish to her temper. She sat still at her desk for a full hour after Matheson had left her, eating chocolates, breaking pencils, and dreaming of revenge.

As it neared twelve o'clock and Molly realized she had accomplished absolutely nothing, she shook herself out of her enraged torpor. Her temper was too great to allow her any trace of efficiency. She had no choice but to seek her usual panacea to depression and frustration.

"I'll be taking the rest of the day off," she informed her curious secretary as she headed out the door.

"Matheson was a bit rough," Betty, a motherly soul in her late fifties, consoled her as she dragged her attention from the typewriter. "You shouldn't let him get to you. You know as well as I do that by next week you'll be his darling golden-haired girl again—his moods never last long."

"I know," Molly said frankly. "It's only when he's right that it bothers me. And I'm afraid he was right this time. If I'd been in control, Elliott would never have got that painting. Or the dry sink, or the pewter."

"Cheer up," said Betty with ready sympathy. "Everyone meets their nemesis occasionally."

"James Elliott is not my nemesis!" Molly snapped, incensed. "He's a gnat, a minor irritation, a flea. As soon as I figure out how to defuse him, he'll prove as harmless as the dud he is. In the meantime—"

"In the meantime you'd better keep away from him until Dr. Matheson gets over his latest tantrum," Betty warned, accustomed to Molly's occasional flare-ups. "You know the old man doesn't like his orders thwarted."

"Yes, ma'am," Molly murmured, her temper, like a falling star, burning out abruptly. "I'll be at Swensens, and then I'll be wandering around the galleries, looking for something to cheer me up. I should be back at my apartment for dinner if anyone needs to get in touch with me."

"Don't wear yourself into a frazzle," her secretary warned.

She may as well have saved her breath. Swensens was the most elegantly equipped gymnasium in the Bay Area. Two hours later Molly was dripping with sweat, her muscles trembling, her heart pounding, the blood pumping through her veins, as she stumbled toward the showers. Two hours of working out, of romping around the various pieces of gymnasium equipment, of skipping rope, of lifting weights, left her feeling completely drained of everything but a glow of physical accomplishment. Lucia had shuddered when she first heard that Molly actually pumped iron, but Molly had steadfastly ignored her arguments. The soft roundness of her upper arms could harden quite effectively into small, hard muscles, and as she sweated and panted and strained Molly envisioned the delightful prospect of punching James Elliott out when next she saw him.

The shower went a long way toward restoring her failing equilibrium, and with renewed vigor she embarked on her next step toward peace of mind.

The trust fund left by Sarah Beaton McDonough was substantial, as befitted the daughter of Jepthah Beaton, inventor of a small, ridiculous ring of metal that had since become a necessary part of most lawn mowers. Molly did her best to leave the legacy alone, supporting herself on her meager salary from the museum. It was only on occasions such as this that she dipped into the considerable assets at her fingertips. A present for herself and her apartment would take her out of her doldrums. A perfect old quilt, whose stitches withstood the test of time, perhaps. Or a primitive painting—one of those solemn little children whose faces had been added belatedly to the stilted bodies painted by itinerant artists during the off-season in the eighteenth and nineteenth centuries. Or an old kitchen table, its surface white from years of scrubbing. The possibilities were endless, and Molly was actually smiling as she began her rounds of the antique shops where she was a well-known figure. James Elliott and his perfidies were banished from her mind.

She had almost decided on a child's rocker, carved by some frontier father more than a hundred years ago, when a beautiful Pennsylvania Dutch paint-decorated dower chest caught her eye.

"How beautiful!" Molly breathed, momentarily entranced, the child's rocker forgotten. It was a beautiful washed-out turquoise, with painted panels of birds and flowers—symbols of hospitality and fertility, abundance and plenty.

"You like that, do you?" Mark de la Ville, the slightly fey owner of De La Ville, Ltd., was hovering by her shoulder. "I almost called you when I first got it in. It seemed just your sort of thing, dearie. All those rampant fertility signs." His bright eyes were maliciously amused.

"And what makes you think I'm in need of fertility signs, Mark?" she shot back, unfazed, as she threaded her way to the chest.

"Not in need of them, M. L.," he purred. "You always struck me as alarmingly fecund. No, I just thought it an apt piece for you and that charming apartment. It's a pity that it's not to be." He shrugged with a Gallic touch surprising in someone whose ancestors had left France over two hundred years ago.

"It's sold?" she wailed, running a delicate, reverential finger along its solid lines.

"It's sold," he verified. "And if it were anyone else, I'd gladly forget my promise and allow you to outbid him, but I'm afraid—" Once more he shrugged, and Molly sighed.

"I couldn't let you do that, Mark," she said seriously. "It wouldn't be fair to your buyer. I'm sure he loves it just as much as I do. I only wish..." Her voice trailed off as a sudden, horrifying suspicion entered her mind. "Mark, who's buying this chest?"

"Now, M. L., you know I couldn't possibly divulge that information," Mark hedged coyly.

"You certainly can," she corrected him. "You've done it often enough in the past. Come on, Mark darling, be a pet. Who is buying it?"

"It won't do you any good to know, M. L."

"Let me be the judge of that," she said inexorably. "Who is it?"

Mark sighed, raising his hands in defeat. "A collector named James Elliott."

Molly straightened up, a determined glint in her blue eyes. "I'll pay you double what he's paying you."

Theatrical regret darkened Mark's freckled face. "If only I could, M. L. You know I'd love to do you a favor."

"Three times what he's paying," she said unflinchingly.

"M. L., you make me blush," Mark protested. "But you must realize I have my honor as a dealer. I couldn't betray my trust for something as sordid as cash."

Molly read with perfect clarity the nuances in his light voice. She hadn't spent years in the art world for nothing, despite Matheson's current contention that she was inexperienced. "What is it you want, Mark?"

He looked pained at her blunt tone. "M. L., couldn't you be a bit more delicate?" he complained.

"No. What do you want for the chest?"

All affectation dropped from Mark, and he became the astute businessman that was his alter ego. "The last price you mentioned was very tempting," he allowed. "And you know as well as I do that it's more than worth it. But I want something else to comfort me for my shattered reputation."

Molly waited, calmly and patiently, knowing he would come to the point eventually.

"I want your pie safe," he said abruptly, and Molly experienced a sharp twinge. Of all the things he could have asked for, he had to choose her favorite piece of furniture in her entire apartment, though certainly not the most valuable. It had been her first purchase when she'd left Sebastian and moved into her apartment, and it represented her pride and independence. Her lips began to form a regretful no, when James Elliott's pale gray eyes floated into her mind, their expression mocking.

"It's yours," she said abruptly, before she could change her mind. "How soon do you want it?"

"I can have my boys deliver the chest and pick it up this afternoon," he said quickly, obviously similarly concerned about her decision.

But Molly had no intention of changing her mind at this point. "That would be perfect," she said, drawing her checkbook out of her purse. "I'll be waiting for you."

That night as she sipped cream sherry and eyed the blanket chest that now replaced her treasured pie safe in the place of honor in her white-painted living room, the unholy glee that had filled her for the last few hours bubbled forth once more.

"And whoever said revenge isn't sweet?" She chuckled to herself. "It's downright delicious!" She raised her sherry glass toward the blanket chest in a silent, delighted toast.

Chapter Seven

Things were disappointingly quiet during the next week. Molly's wicked glee faded to a quiet complacency interspersed with an occasional entirely random chuckle.

James Elliott appeared to have vanished off the face of the earth. Tentative questions, delicately phrased, availed Molly absolutely nothing. A small, craven part of her hoped he would never resurface, a large, wiser part of her breathed a sigh of relief that she might not have to bother with him again. Any other emotions such as disappointment, regret, and longing she ignored steadfastly. If James Elliott had left the Bay Area, then it had to be all for the best, and she could go back to enjoying the even tenor of her pleasant life.

By Friday the worst of her impatience had passed. Lucia was sitting across from her desk, regaling her with ribald tales of her latest young man, a handsome stockbroker named Ian Henderson, as she shuffled a pile of surveys in her crimson-tipped fingers. When the phone rang, the same small clutching of Molly's heart and the speeding up of her pulses alerted her to the fact that she hadn't quite put Elliott out of her mind.

"Hold on a moment, Lucia." She reached out a tanned, deceptively slender arm for the telephone. "Ms McDonough," she answered it, only the slight breathiness in her efficient voice giving a clue to her agitation.

"Hello there, Ms McDonough herself," her father's jovial voice boomed back, and all the tension left Molly's shoulders as she leaned back in her chair.

"Hi, Daddy," she replied, her voice warm and loving. "How are you? I haven't talked with you since you came back from Oregon. How's Elinor?" She prided herself on the casual friendliness of her tone.

Her father accepted it at face value. "She's fine, Molly, and sends you her best love. And I'm fine. As a matter of fact, we're both positively splendid. I was calling to ask if you'd come up to Oregon with me tomorrow and spend the weekend with us. Meet the rest of Elinor's family, get to know her a little better."

Remembering all too well their stilted previous meetings, Molly quickly cast about in her mind for an excuse. Failing to find one, she did the next best thing and lied. "I'm terribly sorry, Dad, but I can't possibly. I promised Lucia I'd help her move."

"Lucia's moving?" Charles McDonough had met and liked Molly's irrepressible co-worker, falling under her spell as quickly as any other man to come within her sphere of influence. "But that's awful! Won't you be missing her, not having her in the same building?"

Never lie when you can be caught out so easily, she reminded herself disgustedly. "Well, actually, it's not Lucia who's moving, it's a friend of hers." She ignored Lucia's expression of cynical amazement.

"Well, can't you tell this friend of Lucia's you have something more important to do?" he demanded somewhat irritably. "You always have some excuse when Elinor invites you up."

"I'm sorry, Daddy," she said meekly, and she was. "But I can't make it this time. Is there... is there any reason why this weekend is more important than any other?"

She heard her father's unaccustomed hesitation, and her heart sank. "I don't think the telephone is any place to discuss it," he said uncomfortably, his voice strained. "Could you meet me for lunch?"

Molly was anything but obtuse. Swallowing the very large lump that had appeared out of nowhere to lodge in her throat, she summoned all the brightness and real joy that she felt. "I'm very happy, Daddy. For both of you. Have you set a date yet?"

"Molly!" her father protested. "This isn't how I wanted to tell you."

"I've known since I met Elinor that she was perfect for you, and I'm very, very glad. You deserve the very best, and I think Elinor will be just that." She cleared her throat, and if her eyes were bright with unshed tears, only a concerned Lucia was witness. "Listen, I can't spare a moment today, but I want to take you out to celebrate when you come back."

"Uh... Elinor will be coming back with me, Molly. She'll have some shopping to do, plans to make. We have to see about selling..." His voice trailed off guiltily.

"Selling the town house?" she finished evenly, ignoring the pang. "That's probably a good idea. Are you planning to live in Oregon or get another place in the Bay Area?"

"Damn it, Molly, this can wait till we have some time alone!" he protested.

"Nonsense. Whatever you decide, I'm behind you a hundred percent. Give Elinor my love, and I want you both for dinner when you get back. I've got a new chest that I think you'll love."

"You know, Elinor has a great fondness for Early American furniture," Charles offered helplessly.

"Does she?" Her voice's usual huskiness disguised the slight coolness. "Why don't you both come Wednesday, and I'll show you my latest treasure?"

"Molly, are you certain?" her father queried, longing for reassurance but not daring to take it.

"I'm positive. Give Elinor a kiss for me and tell her I'll see her Wednesday."

Slowly, gently, she replaced the phone in its cradle, looking up to meet Lucia's sympathetic brown eyes. "They're getting married?" she questioned unnecessarily.

Wordlessly Molly nodded. "I'm being foolish," she added suddenly, the tears still bright in her eyes. "She's absolutely wonderful for him; a sweet, warm, uncomplicated lady with brains and charm and joie de vivre."

"And you hate her guts?" Lucia supplied, used to jealous women.

"Not really. As a matter of fact, I like her quite a lot. She's exactly the sort of woman I used to day-dream about when I imagined my birth mother. Someone warm and giving. But I guess it all boils down to the fact that she's stealing the first and most important man in my life. Freud rears his ugly head and all that."

Lucia considered this. "It's perfectly natural," she decided. "You don't really resent her. You've said many times how great she is for your father. You'll just have to get used to sharing him all over again."

"What do you mean, all over again? I never had to share him before. He and Mother were more like strangers—I always had his undivided love and attention." With a small self-deprecating laugh, she shook her head. "I'll get over it, don't worry."

"I'm sure you will. Especially when you see how happy your father is. Speaking of sharing old loves, guess who's back in town?"

"James Elliott?" she queried, her tongue unguarded.

Lucia stared at her in speechless amazement. "What in heaven's name does James Elliott have to do with old loves? Or have I missed something crucial along the way?"

Molly knew her pale complexion had flushed becomingly, but she did her best to brazen it out. "He must be someone's old love, though I can't imagine who'd be foolish enough to take him. Not that he's not handsome enough—but he has the personality of an adder."

"Oh, I'd put up with a great many snakelike quali-

ties for a face like that. Not to mention his body."
Lucia smacked her lips.

"Lucia, you're incorrigible. Anyway, he's the only
person I know who's out of town on mysterious business. If you didn't mean Elliott, who were you talking
about?"

"Sebastian Coddaire."

"Damn!" Molly swore. "That's all I need. I'm not
in the mood for another trauma. Ex-lovers are low on
my list of desirables at the moment. I don't suppose
he's only passing through?"

"I don't suppose so. I heard from Barry Feinham
that he's looking for a place to stay—one with good
light. I guess he's planning to get fairly entrenched.
He has a show coming up in early December at the
Feinham, so I imagine we won't see the last of him
before the new year."

"Damn," she said again, leaning back in her chair
and wishing she hadn't finished that box of chocolates. "Do me a favor and try to divert him if he
seems headed in my direction. I don't really feel able
to cope with any more hassles at this point in time."

"I can't say as I blame you, but I'm not certain
you'll have any choice in the matter," Lucia said
wryly. "I hear someone coming down the hall in quite
a rage, and I have an uncomfortable feeling it might
be the adder himself."

"God, no!" Molly pushed back her chair, ready to
run, but it was too late. Her door slammed open, and
James Elliott stormed in, all six feet of him in a towering, bristling rage. Molly considered diving under her
desk and hiding in the knee hole, where he couldn't

reach her, then thought better of it. She couldn't allow either Lucia or the adder himself to see how he intimidated her.

Lucia had risen swiftly to her feet, never looking more greyhound-elegant. "Don't go, Lucia!" Molly said swiftly, not caring if it sounded desperate.

Elliott ignored her plea. With one terse jerk of his dark head he ordered Lucia from the room. Without a word, Lucia went, giving Molly a sympathetic little shrug and smile as she silently closed the door behind her.

James Elliott's anger was a formidable thing to see. Not that she hadn't experienced it before—the night of Jeremy Cabello's opening at the Feinham Gallery would be forever emblazoned in her mind. But then ignorance had protected her from being too frightened. The more she knew James Elliott, the more she realized how very intimidating he and his temper were. And she, poor foolish mortal, had deliberately twitched the tiger's tail. It was little wonder those smoky gray eyes smoldered angrily.

Molly was nothing if not foolhardy. Swallowing her sudden panic, she rose gracefully, a distant smile playing about her mouth. "Mr. Elliott," she cooed. "What an unexpected surprise. Did we have an appointment?"

He stopped in front of her desk, three feet of cluttered antique mahogany protecting her from his ire. "You conniving, double-dealing, devious little wretch." He bit each word off. "I'm as unexpected as death and taxes. What the hell did you mean by stealing that chest from me?"

Molly found she could be quite bold with those three feet of desk protecting her. She opened her wide blue eyes even wider in seeming innocence. "Stealing? I have no idea what you're talking about. I did happen to buy a blanket chest last week sometime, but I assure you I did pay for it, and quite an exorbitant amount. Mark de la Ville mentioned he had an earlier offer—" She paused, wrinkling her forehead in pretty confusion. "Oh, dear. Don't tell me you're the one who made the previous offer? But I can see by your fury that you are. What a shame. But then, these things do happen in the art world. It's happened to me several times in the last few months, so I understand how disappointed you must be feeling." Her husky voice consoled him, her eyes mocked him.

He continued to glare at her, and she could almost imagine how much he longed to strangle her with those large beautiful hands of his. Funny, when had she become so obsessed with a man's hands before? They looked strong but gentle, capable of cruelty and great tenderness. He could...

His voice broke through her unexpectedly erotic reverie. "Your sympathy, though charming, is totally unnecessary. All you have to do is sell me *my* blanket chest. The museum shouldn't want it—they already have a superior example of that style and period. I can't see how Matheson would condone wasting funds on an act of petty revenge."

Molly's smile deepened triumphantly, and the one dimple made an enchanting appearance. "I'm certain he wouldn't. But it just so happens that I bought the blanket chest for myself. I don't happen to have another one, and I'm quite pleased with it.''

"If you'd hoped to faze me, you're doomed to disappointment," he shot back. "That's just the sort of thing I expected from you. Name your price."

"I don't have one," she replied sweetly.

"I take leave to doubt that, but it's neither here nor there. Your petty income could hardly compete with the Seaqist millions," he snapped. "How much did you pay for it?"

She hesitated for a moment, her eyes scanning him meditatively. He was even better-looking than she remembered, she realized with a hopeless little pang. During his absence he'd acquired a new layer of tan, and his high cheekbones and arrogant nose stood out sharply beneath the tightly stretched golden skin. The mouth was a thin, angry line, but for some reason Molly wasn't immune to its sensual potential.

"How much?" he repeated impatiently, his flinty eyes meeting hers for a long, breathless moment.

Leaning her shoulders against the wall, she considered her options with maddening deliberation. Instinct and training had taught her never to reveal how much she paid for a particular piece, but more than anything she wanted the arrogant man in front of her to know to what lengths she'd go to best him. Smiling sweetly, she told him.

This time he did look shocked, an emotion he quickly masked. "You paid that much?" he demanded, obviously horrified. "Are you out of your mind?"

"No," she replied, suddenly wondering if she was.

"And I also had to throw in my nineteenth-century pie safe before Mark would agree." She pulled away from the wall, her eyes shooting sparks, her lazy smile vanishing. "It was my favorite piece, and I traded it gladly."

He shook his dark head wonderingly. "You must hate me very much."

"Not really." Where were her reserves of calm when she needed them? Her knees were trembling, and her palms were sweaty. "I just don't happen to like being bested—by anyone, and particularly not by oversexed robber barons!"

Now what had possessed her to say that? she wondered in futile panic as a sudden glint filled his eyes. It was like waving a red flag in front of a bull. "Well, that's a change," he said softly. "First I'm light in the pants, then I'm sex-obsessed. You should get your stories straight, Molly."

The sound of her name, the pet name only her father used, coming from this man's lips only minutes after her father had announced his forthcoming remarriage was more than she could take. "Don't call me that!" she cried.

"And what will you do if I do, Molly?" he drawled, moving around the desk purposefully. "How do you intend to stop me from saying or doing anything I damn well please? You've taken your best shot, and I admit I was annoyed. But there's really not much you can do to stop me from getting my own way. I can be very determined."

He was advancing with agonizing slowness. The typewriter stood beside her desk, cutting off any chance of escape from that side, and he was closing in on the right. She considered climbing over the desk and escaping that way, but the loss of dignity, not to mention grace, was too much to consider. She could always scream for help—Betty was doubtless waiting breathlessly on the other side of the door and would come to her rescue. Molly looked up into James Elliott's smoldering gray eyes as he advanced on her, and considered the horrifying possibility that she didn't want to be rescued.

"And in getting your own way you just ignore any poor fool who has the temerity to get in your way?" she goaded him. "Ride roughshod over everyone else?"

"That's about it," he agreed. There was a small space left between her back and the wall, but she was determined not to cower anymore. She wasn't given much of a chance. Before she could utter another word, those beautiful hands reached out and caught her upper arms. She found her back up against the wall she had avoided, his hard, masculine body pressing against her soft, feminine roundness, making her fully aware of his incomprehensible attraction to her. That he *was* attracted to her, his body left no doubt. Neither did his mouth as he bent down and kissed her, full on her mouth, which was opened in a vain protest.

It was her only attempt at resistance. One arm had captured her shoulders, holding her firmly in place; the other slid down to press the small of her back, tracing slow, erotic designs with his fingers as his tongue caught hers, exploring the sweet wonder of her pliant mouth. And suddenly the hunger that she held so firmly in check broke through, and her tongue met his, no longer shy and retreating, as her arms curled up around his neck and her full, lush hips pressed against his fiery need.

Before she could lose the last vestige of control, however, he pulled away, breaking the embrace with an abruptness that left her mute with shocked longing.

He was the first to speak. His breathing was rapid, and the expression on his usually aloof face was both surprise and a certain smug satisfaction. "Well," he said meditatively, and Molly might have imagined the slight shakiness in his drawled voice. "That was certainly quite a response for a woman who's turned her back on tawdry sex."

Her face, pale from the aftermath of that devastating embrace, darkened with color. "Celibate doesn't mean frigid, Mr. Elliott. I'm a normal woman, capable of normal responses—"

"I'll say," he muttered.

She ignored his interjection. "I just happen to believe in choices, and my choice right now doesn't include you or any other man."

He raised a winged eyebrow sardonically. "Have I misunderstood? Does your choice include women at this point?"

"Don't be ridiculous!" she snapped. "Men like you make me sick. If a woman doesn't fall at your feet, you immediately assume they're frigid or gay. Well, James Elliott, I am neither. I am simply, totally uninterested in you and your attentions!" This stout denial ignored the evidence of her sparkling eyes, the soft mouth still tremulous from his kiss, the way her body yearned to feel his hard, muscled heat against hers once more.

Elliott seemed unmoved by her denial. "Completely immune, eh?" he murmured. "Come to dinner with me tonight and prove it."

"I will not."

He held up his hands in a gesture of surrender. "I swear, I have no ulterior motives. I have to talk you into letting me have the blanket chest."

A mirthless laugh escaped her. "It would be a complete waste of time. You'll get that blanket chest over my dead body."

"Oh, I won't have to go that far," he replied serenely. "I think you should come with me as a reward for my charm and forbearance, not to mention trust. It's not every man who'd take being abandoned so forgivingly. This time, however, we'll take *my* car."

"No, thank you. Although your self-assurance is tempting. You should realize I'm not the sort to let a little thing like a car's ownership stop me if I want to leave."

"And why should you want to leave? Why did you run off like a frightened rabbit in the middle of a very pleasant evening?" He seemed genuinely puzzled. Molly was not about to enlighten him.

"That will give you something to think about during your long, lonely nights," she shot back.

"My nights are neither long nor lonely," he said calmly. "So you really are too scared to come out with me tonight?"

She refused to be baited. "That's as good a reason as any, as long as you accept it."

Shrugging, he tipped his head to one side. "I suppose there's nothing left for me to do but slink away in defeat."

"I suppose so."

"Aren't you going to kiss me good-bye? I thought that was your usual response when angry men barge up to you and kiss you." There was a devilish glint in his eyes.

"Only the first time. By the second kiss they're on their own." The words were out of her mouth before she realized how provocative they were, and it wasn't the first time during this bizarre confrontation.

"Or is it that you just don't dare?" he murmured. "Never mind, Molly Bloom. I'll take care of it."

With a gentleness in direct contrast to the previous fury of his kisses, he pulled her unresisting body into the warm haven of his arms. The lips that brushed hers were warm, wet, and incredibly tender. He trailed a sweet path across her cheekbones, tracing a pattern around her tremulous mouth. Her eyes closed, and she could feel those reverential lips press each fluttering eyelid before returning to the hungry warmth of her mouth to stay. He kissed her, long and slow and deep, until she was trembling in his arms. And then he pulled away, slowly, gently, reluctantly, a warm smile in his usually frosty gray eyes.

"See ya," he said softly, and left her, leaning against the wall for support, staring after him bemusedly.

"Well, well," she whispered.

Chapter Eight

All in all, it had been a hell of a day, Molly thought as she staggered out the back entrance to the Museum of American Arts and headed toward her battered old Peugeot. She felt tossed about and buffeted by emotions completely beyond her control, and at that moment all she wanted to do was drive home as fast as her ancient chariot and the rush-hour traffic could take her, stopping long enough to pick up a good bottle of wine and something heavenly from the German delicatessen near her apartment.

She made it home in record time, a bottle of Bardolino under one arm, a generous portion of sauerbraten under the other. As she started up the stairs to her apartment the muffled strains of Wagner drifted down toward her unwilling ears. A hideous sense of foreboding filled her, and she stopped dead on the stairs, clutching her food to her in panic.

"No," she breathed. "It couldn't be." Determinedly she shook her curtain of blond hair. "No, of course not." She continued up the stairs, but as she neared her door the music grew louder and her steps grew slower. "It couldn't be," she whispered again with renewed desperation. Fate couldn't be so cruel. But deep in her heart she knew it was.

"M. L., my sainted angel!" Sebastian Coddaire boomed at her over the deafening strains of *Die Walküre*. He leaped up from the sofa, knocking over an almost empty bottle of Chablis that only this morning had rested safely in Molly's wine cabinet. Sebastian's feet were bare, and his purple shirt was unbuttoned to the waist, exposing a vast expanse of burly, red-matted chest. His shaggy hair and beard were longer than she remembered, the brown eyes just as soulful as he scampered across the room toward her stunned figure with a grace unusual in a man of his bulk. Before she could gather her horrified wits, she found herself crushed in a bearlike embrace, the sauerbraten threatening to ooze over between the two of them. In time she ducked her head, and his wet, open mouth landed just below her ear.

It took both elbows and one knee to dislodge him. When she finally pried herself free, she headed toward the stereo, turning it off with a decisive click. Taking a few deep, calming breaths, she put the wine and sauerbraten down on the littered coffee table, now covered with candy wrappers, scrunched-up napkins, half-empty glasses, and various other bits of flotsam and jetsam that always seemed to follow in Sebastian's wake. Turning to face her unwelcome guest's puppy-dog expression, she kept a stern face.

"How did you get in here, Sebastian?" she asked severely. "And, for that matter, what are you doing here?"

Sebastian's ruddy complexion took on a mournful cast. "M. L., you wound me! Who else would I turn to in my hour of need?"

"Who else, indeed," she echoed caustically.

"Your landlady let me in, bless her heart," he added piously, a bit daunted by her cool reception. "I told her I wanted to surprise you." Sensing her disapproval, he headed over to the coffee table and began an ineffectual stab at cleaning up the mess he'd left.

"You certainly did that." Her voice was cool.

Sebastian straightened to his full six and a half feet. "Oh, M. L., my sainted angel, I must have hurt you more than I ever guessed! If only I'd known when I left you that you'd take it so hard—"

"When *you* left *me*?" Molly echoed, too astounded to do more than stare at the combination of contrition and smugness that played across his bearded face.

"I haven't been completely out of touch with the Bay Area art world, dear girl. I know that you've steadfastly refused to become involved with a new man, and it's grieved me, grieved me terribly." He looked more pleased than grieved. "You never struck me as one to become bitter."

Molly's mouth opened and closed helplessly a few times as she struggled with the thousand and one outraged protests that warred for expression. In the end she let her fury die away. Sinking into her chair, she allowed exhausted mirth to take over instead. Her laughter rang out through the room.

"Dear Sebastian," she managed after a moment, wiping her streaming eyes. He was staring down at her, deeply affronted, and a small pang of guilt filled her. Yet she had no choice but to make him see reason. "I promise you, I'm not bitter. As I remember our parting—" She stopped for a moment, recognizing his fragile male ego, and quickly amended her original thought. "As I remember, we *both* agreed to part company. It was a mutual decision. You didn't hurt me, Sebastian, and I haven't been in mourning for our relationship. I just haven't found anyone I've wanted." Too late she realized how he could misconstrue that, and he leaped on it like a spaniel on a quail.

"Of course you haven't, dear girl. You may as well accept the fact that we were made for each other. I'm sorry I had to leave you, and I can't promise that I won't have to again. I serve a higher mistress than you, love. But I'll always come back to you," he declared nobly, blithely ignoring the truth of their breakup and the horrified expression on her face.

"Like a bad penny," she muttered under her breath, as, unconcerned, he dived for her dinner.

"Sauerbraten." He sniffed disapprovingly. "You know I can't stand German cooking." He eyed the new bottle of wine with more favor.

"Well, I was hardly expecting you."

"Not to worry." He waved one beefy hand airily. "This will do for tonight, along with one of your sensational mushroom omelets. I've been absolutely starving, waiting for you to come home. All I could think of the past few days was the glorious food you used to cook for me. I'm going to love being back here."

"Really?" Molly was torn between temper and appalled amusement. Had she really ever been in love

with this overgrown, egocentric baby? And then she
looked at his painting of the madonna and child on
her west wall and realized that, yes, she had been. But
now she was finally smart enough to know the difference between the measure of a man and his art.
Thank heavens, she added silently.

"I made a small shopping list for you, M. L.," he
continued blithely. "Just a few of the basic necessi-
ties. I'd offer to do it for you, but I won't have a moment to spare tomorrow—too bloody many things to
do." Although Sebastian was born in Cleveland, he
loved to affect British and French mannerisms, particularly when trying to get his own way.

"What sort of things do you have to do, Sebastian?" she queried, almost afraid to hear the answer.

"I've got to get my work space set up," he replied
testily, obviously annoyed that he had to explain such
simple matters to her. "We'll have to get rid of all this
Early American claptrap. No quilts on the walls, or
blanket chests, or baskets with holes in them."

Molly's depression blossomed like a hothouse flow-
er. "Why, Sebastian?"

"Don't be obtuse, darling girl. This is quite obviously the only suitable room for my studio. Neither of
the bedrooms have adequate light. You can turn the
guest bedroom into a sitting room if you like," he
added magnanimously. "You can even have the
damn idiot box in there, though I don't know if I can
bear having a television in my house. I may have to
insist you get rid of it. That constant chatter can be
very distracting to an artistic mind."

The time was well past for Molly to put a stop to

these fantasies. "Sebastian, you cannot possibly move in here," she began somewhat desperately.

"Don't be ridiculous, M. L. Of course I can." He calmly overrode her protest with his usual single-mindedness. "It's no trouble at all, I assure you. It will all work out fabulously, you'll see. I need a place to work; you have the place. I need to concentrate all my energies on getting ready for my next showing, and you can take care of all the mundane details that are so distracting, such as getting meals together, shopping, all the sort of stuff you do so well." He smiled endearingly. "You know, I've never accomplished as much in as short a period of time as during those two years we lived together. And I don't need to mention that we're dynamite in bed together," he added with a pleased expression.

That wasn't exactly the way Molly remembered things, but she made no comment. Sebastian in bed was very much like Sebastian out of bed—enthusiastic, energetic, and appallingly selfish. She had little doubt his productivity had declined since she had left him; she used to wait on him hand and foot, and enjoyed doing so, feeding his body and his ego with equal fervor.

"That may be, but I don't want you moving in here. I've worked hard to earn my independence, and I don't want to give it up at the drop of a hat."

A mournful expression shuttered his face. "You still aren't ready to forgive me," he announced heavily. "Well, that's all right. When a hurt runs that deep, it takes time to get over it." He sank down on the sofa, its sturdy springs creaking in protest beneath his massive bulk, and he propped his dusty bare feet on the table. "I'm willing to give you the time to realize we belong together."

A wave of relief washed over her. Sebastian could be so awfully single-minded if he chose to be. "Thank you, Sebastian. Time and space are exactly what I need. Where do you think you might stay while you're in the Bay Area?"

"Right here." He leaned back, crossing his arms behind his head.

"Sebastian, no! I told you I need time and space!" she cried, almost at her wits' end.

"And I'll give you time and space. I'll sleep right here on the couch and spend all my time painting," he said in a placating tone. "You'll only be responsible for my meals—otherwise, we don't even have to talk to each other. No, not another word!" He held up a silencing, paint-stained hand. "You're just making up excuses, when you know deep in your heart of hearts you're thrilled to have me back again. Instead of fighting, why don't you see about dinner? I'll open this lovely bottle of wine you bought while you get things going. But don't take too long, will you? I'm absolutely famished."

With a helpless groan Molly rose to her feet. If she listened to one more cheery, egocentric word from her unwanted guest, she would dump the sauerbraten over his shaggy red head. "You can have the sauerbraten," she said sternly, "but you'll have to heat it yourself—I'm not going to wait on you. And you may spend tonight—*one* night—on my couch if you care to. But tomorrow you'll either find a place of your own or another friend to move in on."

"Of course, M. L.," he replied with deceptive meekness, surveying his new home with satisfaction.

Sensing the major warfare that would erupt tomorrow when she actually tried to evict him, Molly decided she needed nourishment. Grabbing the sauerbraten, she headed toward the kitchen, his smug words trailing her.

"You'll see, M. L., this will all work out beautifully," he announced with unimpaired cheeriness. "It'll be just like old times."

"Oh, no, it won't," she swore silently, her back to him. "No, it won't."

Things went from bad to worse that night. Complaining all the way, Sebastian wolfed down the lion's share of the sauerbraten, still lukewarm in its aluminum container, a four-egg omelet that, despite his disclaimers, looked fluffier than any she had ever cooked for him, half a frozen pound cake, the entire bottle of wine, the rest of her bottle of Harvey's Bristol Cream, and was making inroads on her brandy when she finally made her escape. There was a definite amatory gleam in his eyes, increasing as the level of brandy in the decanter decreased, and Molly judged it wise to disappear before he could act upon the impulse. With her door safely locked behind her, she curled up in her large spool bed with its white eyelet sheets, wincing every time she heard Sebastian crash around in the living room. She could hear muffled curses, and had little doubt he'd discovered that she'd removed the plug from the stereo. Wagner at two in the morning, a favorite trick of Sebastian's, was no longer acceptable to Molly.

"Damn," she thought miserably, half a curse, half a prayer. "How am I going to get rid of him?"

There was no immediate answer, only the still-unresolved problems of her wretched day crowding in on her, from her father's incipient remarriage, to James Elliott's demoralizing mouth and lean, elegant, almost sinister body. With a deep groan she pulled one of the plump feather pillows over her head, with the vain hope that it would drown out those disturbing memories as easily as it drowned out Sebastian's nocturnal activities. It was hours before she slept.

Chapter Nine

One advantage with sleepless nights and this apartment, Molly decided groggily, ignoring the distant pounding on her door, was that her bedroom windows faced east, so she could enjoy the sunrises over the rooftops—the glorious gilding of the sky surveyed through sleep-rimmed eyes.

"Wake up, M. L.!" Sebastian thundered against her door, and slowly, reluctantly, she pulled the muffling pillow away and peered at the clock radio beside her bed. Nine thirty. How absolutely splendid—she must have had a total of exactly two hours of sleep. "Go away, Sebastian!" she shouted grumpily. "Leave me alone. Go away and lock the front door behind you."

Her bedroom door rattled ominously beneath Sebastian's hamlike fists. "It's almost ten o'clock, M. L., and I'm starving. Take pity on a poor artist, darling girl. You never used to be so hardhearted." The pounding increased.

The words she muttered under her breath shocked even herself as she struggled out of the tangled bedclothes that attested to her restless night. "If you don't shut up, Sebastian," she called out warningly, "I am going to come out there and shoot you."

Miraculously enough the pounding ceased. Pulling on an enveloping wrapper around her thin silk night-gown, she cast one last, longing look at her bed. But it was too late. She was well and truly awake now, and the sooner she fed the voracious carnivore out there, the sooner she could evict him from her apartment.

When she opened her bedroom door, he was standing there, looming over her, a hurt expression in his eyes and on his petulant mouth. "You shouldn't joke about such things, darling girl," he said sulkily. "How was I to know you didn't mean it?"

"Oh, I meant it, all right," she said blithely as he trailed her into the kitchen. "I just don't happen to have a gun."

With the deftness of long practice she took the coffee beans from the refrigerator, ground them in her electric grinder, and set up the drip pot. "I take it you still like coffee?"

He took a seat at the small butcher block table, leaning back like the lord and master of all creation. "I do. One lump of sugar and only light cream. Milk's too watery, whipping cream's too greasy."

"I have nondairy creamer," she snapped, hoping she could still find the last traces of a jar in the back of her cabinets.

Sebastian was unfazed. "You can add that to the list. I'll have three eggs, sunny-side up. You remember how I like them, don't you, M. L.? The yolks barely cooked, and running when you touch them with a fork. I'd prefer sausage, but I'll take bacon if that's all you've got. You can put sausage on the list too, and oranges. You know fresh-squeezed orange juice is much better for you."

The scream of the tea kettle prevented her from responding to his calmly stated demands, and silently she willed herself to self-control. Taking five eggs from the refrigerator, she began hunting around for her sauté pan, when once more Sebastian spoke up.

"Don't you think you ought to skip breakfast, M. L.?" he questioned kindly. "Or at least make do with just one egg?"

Molly was already famished from her short rations the night before, and the look she turned on Sebastian would have made a wiser man shrink.

"And why should I skip breakfast, Sebastian?" she questioned with deceptive calm, picking up a couple of eggs and rolling them about in her hands meditatively.

Sebastian seemed unaware of his imminent danger. "You know as well as I do that you've put on a bit of weight, dear girl," he said kindly. "I can understand letting yourself go while you've been trying to get over me, but it's time to get yourself back in shape. I want to see you back in designer jeans again. You used to have such a cute little—"

She advanced on him menacingly, ready to crush the eggs into his thick skull, when the doorbell rang. She hesitated, still determined to wreak her revenge, when the bell rang once more.

"I'll be back," she said tersely, a threat, not a promise. Turning, she started out the kitchen, but not before he was injudicious enough to reach out one meaty hand and squeeze her bottom, rather like testing a melon for ripeness.

"Dear, dear, I'd say ten pounds will have to go," he observed cheerfully. "You might as well make it fifteen while you're at it. A woman can never be too thin or too rich."

"I'm going to break your thumbs," she said quite calmly and went to answer the door.

To her complete and absolute horror James Elliott was leaning negligently against her doorjamb, smiling down at her tousled appearance with only a trace of mockery. For the first time he was dressed casually, in faded jeans on his long, long legs, scuffed cowboy boots, a flannel shirt open at the neck to expose a bronzed column of throat, and a wine-colored corduroy jacket over his shoulder. He looked tan and fit and overwhelmingly masculine in the morning light, and all Molly could do was let out a miserable groan.

"That wasn't quite the welcome I expected," he observed sardonically, moving past her into the littered living room.

"I—" Before she could complete her sentence, Sebastian burst through from the kitchen.

"Now, now, M. L., there's no need to be in a huff. I didn't mean to imply that you were fat. Just a trifle..." His voice trailed off at the sight of James Elliott, and a sullen expression came over his face.

It was nothing compared to Elliott's reaction. As his wintry gray eyes took in Sebastian's rumpled appearance, his face and body seemed to freeze before Molly's fascinated gaze, and a look of pure, unexpected, unadulterated anger filled his eyes. And then he swung around to view the littered room, the rumpled couch with its pile of pillows, the empty wine bottles, and the single glass of wine. His shoulders relaxed fractionally.

"Changed your mind, Molly?" he queried softly, and, blushing, she shook her head in silent, angry denial. A small, satisfied smile lit Elliott's somewhat grim mouth, and he nodded.

"Who the hell are you?" Sebastian demanded with his usual bluster.

"James Elliott."

There wasn't much he could do against the short reply, other than blink a few times and mutter "Oh." Marshaling his forces, he tried again. "Are you a friend of M. L.'s?"

"M. L.?" James echoed, momentarily puzzled. "You mean Molly." He cast her a fond look entirely for Sebastian's benefit. "I would certainly say so, wouldn't you, darling?"

She swallowed, then took the cue obligingly offered. "A very good friend," she agreed meaningfully, her eyes warning him that he had better be just that.

She needn't have worried. "Why don't you go and get dressed while Mr. Coddaire and I have a talk. We're supposed to meet Lucia and Ian at ten thirty, and I know you wouldn't want to keep them waiting."

"Lucia and—" she stammered. "Oh, yes, of course. I'll only take a minute."

Sebastian hardly noticed her disappearance, his mind on more important matters. "You know who I am?" he demanded, torn between suspicion and gratification.

"I do, indeed. I've been wanting to talk with you for quite some time now," James said smoothly. "I represent J. E. Seaquist."

"I knew your name sounded familiar!" Suddenly Sebastian was all affability. "Let me get you a cup of coffee—M. L. just made a fresh pot. She's got no real cream, though," he added in an aggrieved tone.

"I'd like that."

Molly listened to their voices trailing into the kitchen with strong misgivings. James was playing with Sebastian, playing on his greed and venality, and for a moment she felt sorry for the artist. And then she looked down at her lush body and hoped James would make mincemeat out of him.

It took her longer than usual to get dressed, a full five minutes of which were spent standing nude in front of the full-length mirror, assessing her body. Her hips were certainly rounder than they had been two years ago, but the skin was smooth and honey-colored, her thighs were firm, her breasts were full but not bloated, and no incipient softness marred her willful chin. If Sebastian still preferred cadavers, that was his problem, she thought, yanking her closet door open with unnecessary violence. And if James Elliott shared that particular fetish, then the hell with him too. But that didn't stop her from discarding three outfits before finally, reluctantly, deciding on the most flattering: a pair of beautifully tailored gray wool pants and a thick Irish fisherman's sweater over a thin cotton shirt. Only the faint mauve shadows attested to her sleepless night, and James Elliott could make what he wanted out of that!

James Elliott was at that moment too busy with other things. As Molly approached the two of them, thick as thieves on the living room couch, she eavesdropped on the conversation with mingled wonder and amusement.

"I agree with you absolutely," James was busy saying. "You can't stay here—you owe it to yourself to have a completely uninterrupted stretch of working time."

Sebastian still looked slightly unconvinced. "But M. L.—I mean Molly—has always been a great help. I'm not sure if she could take being abandoned again."

"Molly will survive. She's a very tough lady, and she'll want what's best for you. It'll hurt, but she'll survive. In the meantime you have to start looking out for yourself, not worrying about everyone else. Your selflessness does you credit, but a great artist can't afford to be a humanitarian. We want to complete the Seaquist collection by Christmas at the latest. Mr. Seaquist's health isn't the best in the world. So you see, time is of the essence."

"You're right!" Sebastian said with sudden decision. "I *have* spent too much time worrying about other people's feelings and not about my art. Could you—could you break it to Molly that I had to leave? I'll just sneak out while you're gone today—I hate tearful partings."

"Count on me," James said solemnly.

Molly deemed it time to break up this touching

scene. "I'm ready," she announced brightly from the doorway. The two conspirators jumped up guiltily, and Sebastian bent an especially fond look at her.

"You look breathtaking, Molly dear," he said warmly. "And I like those trousers—very slimming."

"How kind of you to say so," she replied through gritted teeth. The laughter in James's eyes did little to alleviate her temper, and she all but flounced out of the apartment, ignoring Sebastian's attempts at a properly tragic farewell. It wasn't until she and James were alone on the landing, the door closed behind them, the renewed strains of Wagner echoing forth, that she turned to meet the ripe amusement in his usually aloof face.

"You really were in love with that?" he questioned in disbelief. "I always thought you had such excellent taste. You amaze me, Molly."

"Thank you so much," she said acidly. "As a matter of fact, I discovered toward the end of our relationship that I wasn't in love with Sebastian, and never was. I was in love with his talent. And when I realized I could have his talent without his overbearing presence, I did so."

"He's afraid he's going to break your heart again," he offered solemnly.

"Ha!" Molly's snort was inelegant. "He wasn't able to break it before, he could hardly do so now. Thank heavens you managed to get rid of him. He ignored everything I tried to tell him."

"But you forget, I have a decided advantage on my side," he said coolly. "I simply appealed to his greed."

"The Seaquist millions," she said sharply. "How could I forget? And much as I appreciate your dislodging him, why should it be any concern of yours whether he lives with me or not?"

A sudden, brilliant smile lit his dark face. "Don't be obtuse, darling Molly."

"I didn't realize I was."

He reached out a surprisingly gentle hand and brushed a stray lock of hair out of her eyes. "You look tired," he observed, changing the subject.

"It's little wonder. Sebastian spent the whole night bumping into things."

His eyes fell to her lips. "I trust you weren't one of the things he bumped into?"

"Sebastian spent the night on the couch, and I spent the night locked in my bedroom!" she snapped.

"I know." He nodded easily. "If Sebastian had spent the night in your bed, it would have been much harder to get him to move out. Besides," he added softly as she was pondering this surreptitious compliment, "you still have that determinedly celibate look in your eyes."

"That's good, because I'm still determinedly celibate." Her heart was beating a bit more rapidly than usual, a fact she put down to her frustration over Sebastian rather than James's disturbing proximity. He looked down at her, the amusement in his gray eyes making his usually aloof, elegant face seem almost human.

"Are you?" he murmured softly. "Well, it doesn't worry me."

"Why not?" She was intensely curious.

"Because when you decide to give up your celibate state, I have little doubt I'll be the first to know." Leaning down, he brushed her astonished lips with his own. "Don't be so amazed, Molly Bloom. You'll recognize it sooner or later."

"You—you—" She jerked away from him, starting back toward her apartment. The booming Wagner stopped her in her tracks, and she hesitated, torn.

He had the gall to laugh at her predicament. "You have your choice, Molly. Sebastian Coddaire or me."

Turning back, she faced him unflinchingly. "I'll take you. At least I don't have to wait on you."

He laughed again, and this time she joined him. "Besides, Lucia and Ian will protect you."

"Are we really meeting them?"

"Of course. I never lie," he lied blandly. "Ian's brokerage house handles a large part of the Seaquist estate. I was quite amazed when he told me the beautiful woman he met at a singles bar was none other than your lovely friend. And they do say opposites attract. You two don't have much in common other than your work, do you?"

"Meaning that I'm not lovely?" she said quietly, then wondered what in the world had possessed her to ask such a vulnerable question.

His hands rested lightly on her shoulders, and all laughter vanished from his dark face. "Meaning, Molly Bloom, that Lucia is too free with her favors, and you're too stingy. And the fact that you're deliciously, adorably beautiful only makes matters that much more difficult for your humble servant. However, I'm used to coping with adversity." His hands

dropped from her shoulders and he caught her unresisting hand. "Come along, darling. Lucia's waiting
for us."

And benumbed, she followed.

Chapter Ten

The late afternoon streets were wet and shiny with rain as James deftly drove his jeep toward Molly's apartment, his choice of vehicle one more surprising piece in the enigma that was James Elliott. It had been a perfect day almost until the end, one to make up for the string of disasters that had plagued her yesterday. Lucia's friend Ian had proved to be charming, plain, and bespectacled, and nicer than all of Lucia's one-night stands put together. And Lucia, miracle of miracles, seemed to recognize it.

Of James Elliott's usually mocking demeanor scarcely a trace was seen. He seemed determined to charm all of them, and charm them he did, until even Molly began to relax in his amusing, undemanding company.

He'd chosen a stretch of private beach north of the city for their picnic, and Molly had watched his easy handling of the padlocks and alarm systems on the Hurricane fencing with a trace of her usual misgivings. But the brisk sea air, chilled wine, crusty French bread, cheeses, quiches, tarts, pâtés, and salads were enough to still even the most suspicious mind, particularly when accompanied by a ravenous appetite after her enforced fast. She had even relaxed enough to take a long, silent walk along the rocky beach in his company, while Lucia and Ian whiled their time away, flirting intensely.

He made no move to take her hand, to touch her in any way. He whistled softly as they strolled across the wet sand, their boots leaving sharply delineated footprints in the dampness. The sticky sea spray tangled Molly's hair, clung to her clothes and skin, brought color to her pale cheeks and a sparkle to her smiling blue eyes. Casting a surreptitious glance at her companion's tall, straight, beautifully made body, she marveled that she could be where she was, enjoying herself in this man's company. A week ago, a day ago, she would never have thought it possible. A reluctant laugh escaped her.

"What's so funny?" The question was casual, not aggrieved, and the look he cast her raised her temperature a degree or two.

"I was trying to figure out why I felt so comfortable with you when we weren't saying a word. Usually silences among strangers, or even friends are extremely uncomfortable," she said frankly, scuffing the toe of her leather boot in the sand.

"True enough. Though I don't know if we fit in either category. We're not strangers anymore, and I'm not particularly interested in being tied into the same rigid category of harmless male friend like the rest of your little buddies."

She laughed again, smiling up at him, her dimple

bewitching in her wind-rouged cheek. "And that's exactly why I'm comfortable with you when you don't talk. You have an exceedingly nasty tongue on you, James Elliott."

His smile echoed hers. "Only when I'm trying to keep you off-balance."

"Is that what you're trying to do?" she questioned curiously.

"Of course. You try to render every man you meet into some sort of pallid, inoffensive creature by pigeonholing him in your mind. I'm just making sure I can't be labeled and dissected like all the others."

"I don't do that!" she said hotly.

"Of course you do. You have your tennis-playing banker, your dedicated artists by the score, your slightly malicious antique collectors. Each one is an identifiable type, and each one is completely harmless, in love with his wife, his career, or his own sex."

Molly stopped dead. "Damn you, I knew I shouldn't have come out with you," she spat furiously.

"The truth isn't terribly palatable, is it?" He was completely unmoved by her anger. "Why don't you deny it?"

She stared at him for a long, wintry moment. "Because it's true," she said finally. "Why should I bother to deny it when we both know you're right?" she said, suddenly weary.

He moved closer, his tall body sheltering hers from the wind as he slid one hand behind her neck and pulled her gently closer. "Good girl," he whispered in approval. "I'm glad to see your outrageous honesty extends to yourself."

And, unwillingly but unable to stop herself, she raised her face to meet his kiss, her lips opening to his gently inquisitive mouth. Slowly, tenderly, his lips moved on hers, and she could taste the ocean. Shutting her eyes, she swayed toward him, longing for him to deepen the kiss into one of bone-shaking passion.

But instead, he moved back, and her eyes flew open in surprise and disappointment. The tender smile in his suddenly warm eyes more than made up for the frustrating brevity of his kiss. "It's raining."

She stared up at him blankly, still bemused. "What?"

The smile moved down from his eyes to his mobile mouth. "I said, it's raining. Quite hard, as a matter of fact."

With a startled shriek Molly realized she was rapidly getting soaked. The Irish fisherman's sweater could withstand sea spray but not the heavy, soaking rain that was pouring down. "Well, why didn't you say so?" she demanded irritably.

"I did. You didn't notice." His grin was downright smug by this time, and Molly knew a sudden, overwhelming desire to slap his handsome rain-soaked face. Before she could move he caught her hand, yanking her to run after him along the sand, back to Lucia and Ian and their cars. And she had no choice but to follow—the grip on her wrist was painless but iron hard.

Lucia and Ian had already packed away the remnants of the picnic and were awaiting their arrival in Ian's pale blue Audi.

"We're going out to dinner later after we change," Ian shouted through the downpour as James bundled Molly into the passenger seat of the Jeep. "Want to meet us?"

"Not me," Molly piped up swiftly. "I have too many things to do tonight."

James cast her a curious glance before heading for the driver's side. "Can you give us a rain check, Ian?" He laughed shortly. "Literally."

"Sure thing." The look Ian shared with Lucia left Molly in some doubt as to whether they'd ever make it out to dinner, and a sudden aching emptiness hit her. She knew what it was, of course. A stupid, irrational longing for the joys and torments of being in love, and expressing that love physically. Two years of celibacy were suddenly seeming a great deal longer than they had been before she met James Elliott.

"Could you take me straight home?" she queried in a deceptively polite voice. "I'm soaked to the skin."

He sat beside her, his beautiful hands draped casually on the steering wheel, an enigmatic expression on his face. "All right," he agreed finally. "Whatever you say."

The silent drive back into the city lacked the ease of their walk on the beach, but Molly stubbornly refused to break it. She was just beginning to realize how very dangerous James Elliott was to her, and the sooner she escaped from his admittedly arousing company, the safer she'd be. In the meantime she wasn't about to give him an opening for more of his uncomfortable insights and sexual innuendos that in another man would have made her livid. Not that James Elliott didn't make her livid, but that anger only seemed to inflame the steadily burning coals of her attraction to him.

"Are you certain you want to go home?" His deep-timbred voice broke through her reverie, and she noticed they were nearing her apartment building.

"I'm certain. Why do you ask?"

"Because Sebastian is standing out in the rain, talking with your doorman. If he sees you, he may change his mind about leaving."

Knowing Sebastian of old, Molly immediately slid down in the seat. "Drive by quickly," she commanded in a loud whisper. "I don't want him to see me."

The look he cast down at her scrunched-up figure was vastly amused. "I gathered that much. Where do you want to go?"

"I don't know." Her teeth began to chatter.

"How about this: I'll take you back to my place, where you can have a hot shower and a shot of brandy while I find out what Sebastian's planning to do. I may need to wave the Seaquist money in front of his nose again before he finally decamps."

Molly hesitated for only a moment. Charles's town house was halfway to Oakland—she could hardly ask him to drive her there—and Lucia's apartment would either be locked and empty or put to very private use. "I guess that's the best option," she agreed. A combination of inevitability and nervousness set in, and sternly she banished it. She hadn't yet met a man she couldn't manage. James Elliott was proving to be a particularly difficult case, but she had little doubt she'd handle him in the end. Or did she?

"Look, I'm sure I don't really need a shower," she said, her husky voice betraying her nervousness as she followed him into the apartment. "Just a cup of coffee and a chance to get warm will be more than sufficient."

As he was paying absolutely no attention, she let her words trail off, following him like a docile puppy, she thought with a trace of rancor.

Once again she admired the wide, uncluttered spaces of his apartment, the shiny, beautifully aged hardwood floors, the perfect furniture, the eclectic choice of paintings, ranging from a Canaletto to several impressionists to Sebastian at his most abstract, the choice of which was somehow *right*.

And then her gaze froze as she spied her beloved pie safe. "Where did you get that?" she demanded with well-concealed hostility.

He didn't even bother to turn to see the object of her interest. "Mark de la Ville. He'd been looking out for a pie safe for me for over a year now."

A dreadful, infuriating suspicion filled her. "That wasn't, by any chance, a setup?" Her voice was level, but James wasn't fooled.

He paused by the door on the far side of the apartment, turning to face her accusing glare. "No, it wasn't," he said with great seriousness, then spoiled it all by grinning. "It would have been a great idea, though."

"I don't think so."

"No, you wouldn't. Anyway, much as I wanted your pie safe—and, yes, Mark told me it was yours when I was trying to haggle him down on the price—I would never have given up the blanket chest."

"I don't suppose you'd consider selling it back to me?" she had to ask and was rewarded with a rude laugh.

"As someone so sweetly put it just yesterday, over my dead body. But that's all right, Molly Bloom, you can come visit it any time." He opened the door on a large bathroom.

It was very much like its owner—dark, elegant, and uncompromisingly masculine, from the marble tub to the thick chocolate-brown towels and deep pile carpeting. It was a sybaritic bathroom, and Molly felt her old distrust increase.

"Sorry I haven't got a hot tub; I'd join you," he said, deadpan, and she couldn't tell whether he was serious or not. He handed her a blue silk bathrobe from the brass hook behind the door. "Leave your clothes outside the door, and I'll dry them by the fire."

"What fire?" She caught hold of the silky foulard in nervous hands.

"The fire I'm going to start once you give in and take your shower," he explained patiently. "And if you don't hurry up, you'll catch pneumonia."

"But—don't you need to dry off too?" she stammered. "You're just as wet as I am."

"Why, Molly, is that an offer to share your shower?"

"It is *not*," she snapped. "Go away."

"Yes, ma'am. The fire will be lit and the brandy poured by the time you're finished."

"Sounds seductive," she observed sourly.

"Don't worry your head about it, Molly," he soothed her with a wry grin. "I have remarkable self-control. Your virtue is safe with me." He shut the door behind him as she attempted to throw the robe at his head.

The hot shower was heavenly, and the bathroom door had a sturdy lock. The steady beat of the water on her skin had a soporific effect, and even rubbing a thick, thirsty towel vigorously over her body failed to counteract the effects of too many sleepless nights.

The feel of the cool silk against her bare skin was both sensuous and disturbing. She could smell the woodsy after-shave James usually wore clinging to the silken folds, and even tightly belting the waist and rolling up the overlong sleeves failed to turn the wonderfully elegant thing into an ordinary dressing gown.

She could hear the fire crackling as she cautiously stepped from the bathroom. James was standing by the fireplace, surveying his results with a dubious expression. He'd changed clothes, and the black denims that he now wore hugged his long legs. His feet were bare, his torso covered with an open, untucked white shirt that set off the tanned smooth expanse of his chest. No covering of silky black hair, Molly noticed with an absent pang of lust. Just smooth, tanned, muscled flesh. A small sigh escaped her.

His black hair was still rumpled from a rough toweling, and the eyes that met hers glowed in silent appreciation. "You sure look a hell of a lot better in that bathrobe than I do," he observed.

"I doubt it."

"What's that supposed to mean?"

Molly shrugged. "I can imagine you bought this to look gorgeous for the women you consort with."

"Why, Molly, bless your heart!" he teased. "I believe you just told me you find me good-looking."

"I didn't say anything you didn't know already," she said sourly. "Pretty is as pretty does."

His laugh rang out, his teeth very white in his dark face. "Not up to your usual standards, Molly. You can do a lot better than that in trying to cut me down to size."

"I know." She yawned hugely and unaffectedly. "But I'm too tired to think of anything right now."

"Poor angel." His deep, low voice sent little shivers down her silk-covered spine. "The brandy's on the coffee table. Why don't you curl up on the sofa for a bit while I cope with this fire?"

She shouldn't, she knew perfectly well that she shouldn't. She should sit on that Windsor chair by the fireplace, eschew the brandy, and make polite conversation while her clothes dried. But damn, she was tired.

"All right." She headed toward the sofa that had once been an eighteenth-century bed, the three high sides protecting the sleepers from omnipresent drafts. It felt like a cocoon, Molly thought, curling up against the white pillows and taking a cautious sip of her brandy before tucking her bare feet up under the silk robe and leaning back. James was having a bit more success with the reluctant fire, and as she stared into the yellow and orange flames she felt her eyes drifting closed. For a moment she resisted, and then, with a sigh, she gave in and let sleep claim her.

Her dreams were fleeting, confused, jumbled images. When she felt him sit beside her recumbent body, she knew she should wake up, jump up. But she wanted to stay there, warm and sleepy and sensual, and she willed herself back to sleep. The gentle touch of his hand against her cheek, the fingers trailing down the cord of her neck, caused her to sigh and butt against that hand like a purring kitten.

Lips followed his hand, warm, gently nibbling kisses teasing across her cheekbone and jawline, across her vulnerable throat as his hand preceded them, slipping inside the loose silk robe to cup the soft warmth of her full breast. Instinctively she arched against him, pressing against his hand, as she felt him dispense with the loosely tied belt. The air was warm when it hit her pliant body as he pushed the robe aside, and for a moment her eyes fluttered open, then shut again.

Don't wake up, she told herself groggily. *If you wake up, you'll have to leave this couch, and his hands, and his mouth,* that was trailing sweet, soothing kisses across her heated skin. *Or face the responsibility if you stay.*

The hand that was cupping her breast moved lower, across her softly rounded stomach, leaving a trail of fire as it danced across her hips. Bending his dark head down, his mouth caught her breast, his lips and tongue teasing the tiny nub into aching arousal. Her eyes flew open, unable to find forgetfulness in sleep, as his lips moved back to hers and his hand gently parted her legs, tracing delicate patterns on the soft inner flesh of her thighs.

It was far too late for Molly to protest; her body had taken over, and in her sleep and sensuality-drugged state she could do nothing but arch her hips up against his hand, opening her mouth beneath his gently questing one with a helpless little moan of desire.

His other arm slid around her, drawing her trembling body close against him, as his hand finally reached the damp, heated core of her femininity. With a hoarse cry she pulled her mouth away from his, burying her face against the smooth, hot skin of his shoulder. And as she hid her face against his chest his hand continued its experienced explorations, driving her to the edge of madness, until suddenly, wondrously, her entire body went rigid in his arms, her teeth sank into his shoulder, as wave after wave of unbelievable sensations washed over her. The moment seemed to go on forever, suspended in time, until finally she collapsed, sobbing her release, against him.

His hand left her to reach up and cradle her head against him, James all the time murmuring soft, gentle words of praise and passion. As reality finally began to intrude Molly realized that these were the first words either of them had spoken in the last tumultuous minutes. She slowly lifted her head from its cushion against his shoulder, and her eyes met his.

It was dark in the room by this time, only the late afternoon glow of the setting sun and the dancing flames of the fire illuminating the dark intensity of his eyes as he stared down at her. And then he blocked out the light as he kissed her, slowly, deeply, thoroughly, his tongue teasing hers into complete acquiescence.

And then, to her astonishment, he gently pulled away, leaving the couch to stand and stretch before heading into the kitchen area.

"Would you like some coffee?" he inquired with calm solicitude, switching on a light that flooded a small section of the huge room and blinded her to his expression. He seemed calm and completely unruffled, but Molly knew otherwise. She had felt his racing heart against her breasts, seen the very tangible evidence as he stood, silhouetted against the fire.

Slowly she pulled the silk wrapper back around her body, her hands still trembling slightly from the intensity of her reaction. What kind of game was he playing with her?

"No, thank you," she managed finally, her voice huskier than usual. "I really should be getting home." She waited for his denial, waited, breathless, for him to come back to the couch and finish what he had started. That solid core of desire that had been so recently appeased was beginning to grow again, and she felt suddenly, overwhelmingly incomplete.

"All right." He put up no argument whatsoever, busying himself with filling the tea kettle. "Your clothes should be dry by now. Just give me time for a cup of coffee, and I'll drive you home."

Molly didn't know whether to be hurt, furious, or grateful. He had promised that her virtue was safe from him. But why? He obviously wanted her...why didn't he override her maidenly objections and take her to bed? Damn, she was confused!

Grabbing her clothes from the chair by the fire, she hurried back into the bathroom, yanking them on with trembling fingers. Her eyes were luminous in her pale face as she stared at her reflection in the mirror. Her lips were slightly swollen, her hair a tousled mass around her face. "What the hell is he trying to do to you?" she whispered.

He was sitting on the sofa, his shirt was still open around his bare torso, a cup of coffee in his hand, a meditative expression on his face. He looked up when she walked in, and she could read nothing whatsoever in his face.

"I'll be ready in a few minutes," he said calmly. "Are you sure you wouldn't like a cup of coffee?"

"No, thank you. And if you don't mind, I'd rather you didn't drive me home. I'll get a taxi." She was pleased that her voice matched his for calm.

"Why?"

That was enough to give her pause. "I'd just prefer it," she said finally, waiting for his reaction.

It wasn't what she expected. "If you wish. Would you like me to call you a cab?"

Feeling more and more out of her depth, she shook her head. "That's all right, there are always plenty of them cruising this area." She hesitated, but there wasn't really anything more to say. "Well, good-bye."

He moved then, rising slowly and gracefully from the couch and moving over to her waiting figure with lithe power. His hands cupped her face as he bent down and kissed her, slow, sweet, drugging kisses that

added to her confusion. "I hope you appreciate my
forbearance," he said gently against her trembling
mouth. And he kissed her again before she could reply.

When he finally released her, she was even more
baffled and frustrated than she had been before.
"Good night, Molly," he whispered.

She considered ripping off her sweater and begging
him to take her to bed. She considered kissing his
knees in supplication, bribing him with the blanket
chest, a thousand other things. And then, belatedly,
she remembered just how devious James Elliott could
be.

Holding herself stiffly, she glared at him, managed
a frosty good-bye, and slammed the door quite loudly
behind her departing figure.

James, who had watched the bewilderment, desire,
and rage play across her expressive features, laughed
ruefully. "And that's just the way I want to keep you,
Molly Bloom," he said softly to the closed door.
"Frustrated and confused."

And with that he drained his coffee and headed for
a very long, very cold shower.

Chapter Eleven

"My, my, aren't we in a good mood today?" Lucia purred sarcastically from the doorway of Molly's cluttered office, where she had paused on her way down the sparsely elegant museum hallways. "What's happened to put you in such a jolly mood?"

Slamming shut the heavy tome that had rested, unread, upon the mountainous pile of correspondence on her desk, Molly leaned back and sighed grumpily. "It's nobody's fault but my own," she replied with some obscurity.

"That's usually the case. What's troubling you in particular on this lovely autumn day?"

"My father and Elinor are coming for supper tonight, to celebrate their engagement and to give me a chance to get to know her better," she said morosely.

"What's the big deal? I've seen you manage dinner parties for twenty with only a few hours notice. Or am I missing the point?"

"You're missing the point. The apartment is spotless, the *boeuf bourguignon* and the mocha cheesecake are in the fridge, everything's ready." Her flat tone took no joy in her efficiency.

"And you don't feel ready to cope with your father and his fiancée," Lucia supplied.

"I'm afraid not. I just don't know if I can tap-dance through the evening, all smiles and chatter. It's rotten of me to feel this way, but I can't seem to help myself." Molly managed a rueful smile. "I don't suppose you and whatever young man is currently enjoying your favors would be interested in joining us for dinner? To serve as sort of a buffer?"

"It's still Ian, dear. And much as I'd love to help you out, we're committed to the Oakland Symphony with Ian's senior partner."

"Good heavens, it sounds ominous, Lucia." Molly roused herself from her abstraction. "Meeting his associates, still seeing him after two weeks. Next thing you know he'll have you home to meet his parents."

"Next Saturday," Lucia verified with a grin. "And speaking of which, that's a great idea. Why don't you invite James Elliott for dinner tonight? He'll be enough to distract you from whatever misgivings you have about your future stepmother."

"Are you out of your mind?" Molly demanded, feeling the color flood her face. "I'm afraid that sounds like a case of the cure being worse than the disease."

"I don't see why. The man's attracted to you—any fool can see that," Lucia argued. "And I didn't see you putting up any great fight on Saturday. How long has it been since you've seen him?"

By sheer force of will Molly managed to stem the second rush of color that swept over her face. "Not since the picnic," she murmured. "We went back to his apartment for coffee, and then I went home."

If Lucia suspected Molly was omitting important details, she was tactful enough not to press her. "Well, then, it's your turn to invite him over. You owe him something for having got rid of Sebastian for you. Has he been in touch since Saturday?"

"No."

Lucia shrugged her elegant shoulders. "I think your course is obvious. Invite him for supper tonight."

"And I think you're out of your mind," Molly snapped. "I'd invite—" She cast about in her mind for someone suitably ghastly, and came up with it triumphantly. "I'd invite Sebastian before I'd invite James Elliott."

"Yuk." Lucia's reaction was succinct. "Well, it's your decision. But I wonder if your edginess about tonight isn't perhaps compounded by the fact that James hasn't called in four days."

"Thank you, Dr. Joyce Brothers. Enjoy your lunch." Molly dismissed her.

"Are you sure you don't want to join us? Ian thinks you're charming."

"And I think Ian's charming. But I wouldn't be very good company," she confessed.

"Call him, M. L."

"Go to hell, Lucia," she replied genially.

It took her one hour and forty-five minutes to get

up the nerve to call James Elliott; one hour and forty-five minutes of carefully rehearsed, charmingly brittle imaginary conversation. She had finally settled on just the right approach—a combination of offhandedness and self-deprecating humor—when the sharp buzz of the telephone startled her out of her reverie. James Elliott's cool tones left her momentarily speechless, floundering for words that eluded her.

"Molly?" His reaction to her continued silence was amused irritation. "Are you there?"

She cleared her suddenly dry throat. "Hello, James." Thank heaven her voice came out clear and calm. "I was just thinking of you."

"So I gather" was his dry rejoinder.

"What do you mean by that? Have you become a psychic in your old age?" she shot back.

"I wish I could convince you of that, but even you aren't that gullible. Ian Henderson just called and said you wanted to get in touch with me."

Damn Lucia, Molly thought with sudden rancor. For a moment she considered denying it, then gave in. After all, what did she have to lose? "Now I think it's Ian who's being psychic. I *was* thinking of calling you, but I hadn't quite made up my mind yet."

"And what occasioned all this soul-searching?" James's voice was silk and steel.

Molly took the plunge. "I wondered if you'd care to come for dinner tonight." There was a dead silence on the other end of the line, and she quickly rushed ahead. "I know it's rather late notice, but I'm having my father and his fiancée for dinner, and I suddenly thought I could do with some moral support."

His short bark of laughter failed to reassure her. "I would have thought I'd be more likely to qualify as *immoral* support."

Molly's temper, fueled by a latent embarrassment, flared into a bonfire. "Forget it. I'm sure Sebastian will be available—I've never known him to turn down a free meal. He should be distraction enough."

"Calm down," James soothed her. "If I sounded hesitant, it was only because you caught me off guard. I'd love to come to dinner tonight and distract you— as a matter of fact, I can't think of anything I would rather be doing tonight. I take it you don't approve of the match?"

"You take it wrong. They're perfect for each other. Elinor's charming, and they'll be very happy together," Molly said gloomily.

"So it's simply a matter of an Electra complex. How Freudian of you," he said smoothly. "What time do you want me, my poor little obsessive darling?"

"Very funny," she snapped. "I told them to come around seven."

"All right. I'll be there early and give you a hand."

"There's no need…" Her voice trailed off. James Elliott had already hung up.

"Do I need this aggravation?" she demanded of her reflection in the full-length mirror inside her bedroom closet door. The reflection smiled back, not without a certain saucy charm, and Molly sighed. The sleek, clinging black jump suit hugged her figure, accentuating every ripe curve. A little too ripe, Molly decided. The silky black material might do wonders for James Elliott's sangfroid, but it was scarcely proper for a dinner with her father and stepmother-to-be. Her tumbling mass of blond curls had better be tucked into a discreet French knot, the jump suit traded for something sedate and boring, she decided. She had the long zipper undone when the doorbell rang, and with a muttered curse she pulled it back up again, heading out of her bedroom toward the front door.

As a cruel fate would have it, the zipper stuck halfway up, and all her desperate struggles helped her not one bit. The bell rang again, and as she battled with the recalcitrant zipper her temper broke.

"Hold on a minute," she snapped to the closed door.

"I have a great dislike of standing around hallways like a hopeful suitor, carrying wine and flowers," James Elliott's dry voice filtered back.

"You're early," she said, stalling for time.

"How observant of you. I told you I'd come ahead of time and help you. Are you going to let me in, or are we planning to continue this conversation through the door? If so, you might allow me a chair out here. It's been a long day, and I'm quite exhausted."

"All right, damn you." Twisting the locks with angry force, she flung open the door, holding her gaping cleavage shut with an ineffectual hand.

"Thank you," he said icily, striding into the apartment and looking not the slightest bit exhausted. As a matter of fact, he looked dangerously lively, and Molly pulled the jump suit closer about her.

"Having a problem, Molly darling?" he inquired solicitously, the gray eyes alive with devilry.

"Nothing I can't manage," she said crushingly.

"You don't look as if you're managing so well at this point," he observed. "However, I'll be a gentleman. Where would you like these?" True to his word, he had come equipped with a bouquet of flowers and two rather dusty bottles of wine.

"In the kitchen," she managed. The flowers were yellow sweetheart roses, her favorite, and she wondered once more if James Elliott was psychic, or simply lucky. And then she reminded herself that this wasn't the first time they'd shared the same taste, and it had always been to her detriment. "Thank you for the flowers." Her voice was cool.

His sudden, slashing grin almost demoralized her. She had forgotten how very attractive he was, with his tall, lean body encased in a charcoal-gray suit whose cut proclaimed Europe even to her inexperienced eye. His eyes were both soothing and threatening, and that smile almost destroyed her remaining convictions. "I'm glad you like them. You actually strike me as more of a gardenia type, but I thought you'd prefer something for the table."

"I always pictured a gardenia-type woman as someone dark and sultry and exotic," she said, not denying her love for the pungent bloom. "Not a rounded, blue-eyed blonde."

"Oh, I think gardenias are perfectly suited for a certain sultry, exotic, quite luscious blonde of my acquaintance." His voice caressed the word *luscious*, and Molly felt an answering quiver in the pit of her stomach. "I'll go and put these in water and then I'll help you with that zipper." He disappeared into her kitchen, making himself right at home with an ease Molly should have found infuriating but instead found rather comforting. She knew she should follow him into that compact space, but her stuck zipper was of more immediate importance, and she renewed her struggles with a trace of desperation.

Moments later he was back, his large beautiful hands catching hers and stilling her struggles. "Be calm, Molly Bloom," he murmured gently. "I'll take care of it." And with mesmerizing care he moved her hands out of the way, his own settling deftly on the caught zipper just below her full breasts. But not deft enough. Despite the calm expression on his face, his breathing was slightly forced, and with a sudden rending sound the zipper gave way. Unfortunately, it broke, parting company all the way down her torso, exposing the peach silk-and-lace underwear that barely covered her firm, full flesh.

Before James could react, Molly yanked the jump suit together, her face crimson.

"You needn't look so mortified, Molly," he drawled, apparently unmoved. "I've seen you in far less."

"How dare you remind me of Saturday?" she shot back, fury momentarily wiping out her embarrassment.

"I wasn't thinking of Saturday," he responded lightly. "It was too dark to fully enjoy your many charms, Molly darling. No, I was referring to two rather charming canvases I was able to wrest from Sebastian that now possess a place of honor in my bedroom. I particularly like the second one with you lying on that blue rug, with that to-hell-with-you expression on your face."

"Oooooh!" The rage and fury in that shriek echoed through the apartment, and her hands clenched into fists.

"Is that all you can say?" he mocked. "I would have thought you'd be flattered. I spent quite a bit on them—Coddaire wasn't about to let them go cheaply, especially once he knew how much I wanted them."

"Oooooh!"

He was still unmoved by her impotent fury. "You don't need to worry that they'll go on display. *I* bought them, not Seaquist, and they're for my personal delectation and nobody else's."

All her speechless rage finally erupted into a torrent of words. "You rotten, unprincipled bastard!" she shrieked. "How could you do such a miserable thing? And don't hand me that garbage that no one will see them! The women you seduce are bound to notice them on your bedroom walls—they're larger than life-size."

"Ah, but you forget," he said sweetly. "I use my couch for my seductions, not my bedroom."

Her reply was so obscene, it even surprised her. She repeated it, savoring the sound.

The humor vanished from James's face. "If you say that one more time, I'll wash your mouth out with soap," he threatened sharply.

Smiling sweetly, she said it again, loud and clear, enunciating each syllable with precision as it rolled off her tongue. Before she could say it for a fourth, triumphant time, James caught her around the waist, dragging her kicking, flailing body toward the bedroom.

Chapter Twelve

"You asked for it, Molly," he said grimly, ignoring her struggles. "I won't have you foul-mouthed like your namesake, and I certainly won't have you calling *me* any of those lovely names. A nice rinse with soap should do wonders, and I have little doubt your father will approve."

Grabbing on to the bedroom door, Molly held on for dear life, but with an abrupt jerk, James yanked her free, dragging her past her antique spool bed toward the bathroom. Molly kicked out, her foot connecting quite sharply with his iron shin. Ignoring the pain in her foot, she glowed with satisfaction at his start of pain.

With a word scarcely less obscene than her earlier epithet, he changed course, flinging himself on the bed and dragging her struggling body across his knee. The first swat shocked her into a shriek, the second into silence, the third into tears. By the fifth and final spank she had stopped struggling, and it was with a kind of rough concern that he released her, letting her slide between his knees, holding her there with his leanly muscled thighs as gentle hands pushed her tumbled hair away from her flushed, tearstained cheeks.

"Tears?" he questioned softly. "I didn't hit you that hard."

"I know." It came out as a hiccoughing sob, and with a low murmur he pulled her into his arms, pressing her trembling body against his broad, warm chest. She wept against the soft white shirt, inhaling the clean masculine scent of him, the faint traces of aftershave and pipe smoke, and she had no idea why she wept.

Finally, the tears shuddered to a stop, and she raised her woebegone, tear-streaked face to his. "I've never seen you smoke a pipe," she said absently.

A low chuckle escaped him. "There's a lot you've never seen me do," he murmured and dropped his mouth lightly on hers. His tongue snaked out, gently teasing her vulnerable mouth open to taste the sweet, honeyed warmth that lay hidden. She withstood the gentle assault passively, savoring the feel of him. And then he pulled his mouth away, laughing lightly.

"It's a good thing I decided to spank you rather than wash your mouth out with soap," he said huskily against her lips. "You wouldn't taste half so good with a mouthful of suds. As it is, you're positively delicious." To prove his point he kissed her again, deepening the pressure of his mouth on hers, thrusting his tongue against hers with a demand that denied all her attempts at passivity. And with a low, shaking moan of desire she abandoned her last shred of control, meeting the fiery demand of his mouth fully, holding nothing back as she gave in to the magical touch she had craved since Saturday night and, indeed, if she was honest, from the first time she had seen him.

It was a simple enough matter for his hand to slip inside the wide-open front of her jump suit and dispense with the front clasp of her lacy scrap of bra. His warm strong hand closed over her breast with a rough possession that she reveled in, and she pressed her trembling flesh eagerly against that hand, glorying in its fierce demand. She moaned in disappointment against his hot, questing mouth as his hand left her, only to find the silky, clinging jump suit pushed off her shoulders and down her willing arms. Shoving it down to her hips, James levered his body back across the bed, breaking its seal with hers for a moment.

"James," she murmured, half a protest, half a plea, as he gently, tenderly stretched her out beside him. His hands on her fevered flesh were deft and arousing, pushing the material out of the way of his wetly exploring mouth. Her skin seemed to leap with delight as he trailed kisses across her shoulders, down past her navel to the edge of the jump suit. And then he moved back up, his mouth capturing one aching breast, his tongue gently flicking the nipple into a desperate, burning arousal.

Molly was on fire. Tremors shook her body as she pulled him closer, closer to her straining body, yearning for him to fill that desperate void that longed for him, wept for him. "James, please," she whispered hoarsely, not quite sure whether she was begging for mercy or completion. Perhaps it was the same thing.

James had no such doubts. "Be patient, my love,"

he whispered, moving his mouth to her other breast and capturing it with sudden rough passion. His hands slid down, slipping the jump suit off her lush hips, and she raised herself eagerly, longing to lie naked in his arms, longing for that final completion that she knew would be beyond anything she had ever experienced. She wanted him more than she had ever wanted anyone in her life, and as his hand moved down to the heat of her passion a moan of anguished desire shook her.

The ringing of the door bell cut across her like a bucket of ice water. They both became motionless, listening in stunned disbelief. And then suddenly he released her, pulling himself upright. "I would guess that's your father," he said lightly, his eyes glowing as he stared down at her shamelessly nude body.

"Oh, no," she groaned weakly, rolling over and hiding her face in the pillow, oblivious to the equally charming back view her nude body presented to James's appreciative eyes.

"Oh, no, indeed," he said with a trace of shakiness in his voice. "Don't you think you'd better answer it?"

Rolling back, she glared up at him. "Good grief, you're still dressed!" she realized belatedly, stumbling over to her closet and grabbing her robe from the hook. "You even have your tie on!" she accused him.

"I was busy with other things," he said unrepentantly. "At least it's mussed."

The doorbell rang again, this time more insistently. "Will you get the damn door?" she demanded, harassed, as she belted the robe tightly around her still-aroused body.

"I don't think I'd better."

"Damn it, you're dressed and I'm not!" she cried in exasperation.

"Nevertheless, I'm hardly in any condition to answer the door," he said solemnly, a wicked gleam in his eyes.

"Unless you wish me to do something violent to take care of your...uh...condition," Molly said dangerously, "I suggest you get out there."

"You would, wouldn't you?" he marveled, not at all chastened. "I'd better watch my step around you."

"You betcha." Suddenly a smile burst forth, lighting her face at the bizarre humor of the situation. "For heaven's sake, James, *please* go out there and keep my father and Elinor busy while I pull myself together."

"When you smile like that, I'd do almost anything for you," he said lightly. "Don't take too long."

"I'll try not to," she replied with her customary honesty. "I'm not sure how steady I am."

"That makes two of us. We could always not answer the door..."

Almost afraid to touch him, she reached out and gave his unresisting body a shove through the door. "Forget it."

All in all it was an interesting, surprisingly relaxed evening, Molly realized later. By the time she had pulled herself together, dressing in her most subdued clothing and scraping her hair back from a flushed face that cold water had failed to tone down, James had managed to charm both Charles and Elinor, plying them with drinks and canapés until Molly's belated entrance was almost anticlimactic.

Despite her previous bitchy contention, there was no real resemblance between James and her father. True enough, they were both tall, with Charles's dark hair well-silvered. But where James's face had a distant elegance, an aloof charm, the older man's expression burst with life and gaiety, nurtured by the quiet pretty woman at his side. Elinor was a good match for him, just above middle height, with a slightly plump, rounded body, laughing blue eyes, blond hair fading to gray, and a surprising dimple in her right cheek, in evidence as she smiled to greet her future stepdaughter.

"Molly, my angel!" Charles enveloped her in an enthusiastic bear hug, his delight overflowing as usual. Finally, he allowed her to turn to greet Elinor.

She did so, not without the usual confusing pang as she met her stepmother's warm blue eyes. "How are you, Elinor?" Molly managed an answering warmth. "You look lovely in that shade of green. It's one of my favorite colors."

"It's Elinor's favorite too," Charles boomed, and then looked curiously guilty as the room lapsed into an uncomfortable silence.

Always the perfect hostess, Molly broke the silence. "Well, then, it's probably James's favorite color too, though I have yet to see him in sea green. We have an unfortunate history of sharing the same taste," she said lightly.

Charles laughed, the look of anxiety fading from his brown eyes. "Yes, he told me of your battles. Sounds like my Molly."

"Did he really?" She eyed James curiously, but he was unabashed.

"An expurgated version," he murmured, a strange, abstracted expression in those fathomless gray eyes. "I've been very discreet."

"You'd better warn him, Molly; I'm a protective father," Charles said jovially. "She had to forcibly restrain me from breaking Sebastian Coddaire's nose when she moved in with him. But I've finally learned that children have to make their own mistakes, just like their parents." He cast a fond glance at Elinor, and she smiled back, the two of them sharing a tender, private moment, oblivious to the others in the room.

"I have to get dinner ready," Molly announced in a strangled voice, all but racing to the kitchen. As luck would have it, James was on her heels, shutting the door behind them as Molly did her best to ignore him. The *boeuf bourguignon* was bubbling merrily in the oven, the bread was ready to be heated, and the water was on a low boil for the noodles.

"Well, Sister Molly," James mocked her, "I never thought you could manage such a transformation in that short a time. You look just like a nun. When I think of how you looked, lying on your bed with that vulnerable expression in your eyes..."

"For heaven's sake, stop it!" Molly begged. "I'm having a hard enough time as it is."

"I'm afraid that's more than obvious to your father

and Elinor. You could manage a little better, I think."
There was just a trace of severity in his voice, and
Molly flushed.

"Is it that apparent?" she asked miserably.

"I'm afraid so. You'll have to let go of him sometime, Sister Molly."

Keeping her back to him, she dropped the noodles
into the boiling water. "As a matter of fact, the
strange thing is that I'm jealous of both of them. I
want Elinor to be my stepmother—I've always wanted
someone warm and maternal to be my mother."

"And your adoptive mother wasn't?" he questioned gently.

"Not so you'd notice," she said wryly. "Did you
know Elinor has five children? And somewhere near
a dozen grandchildren, not to mention nieces and
nephews and brothers and sisters. I want to be a part
of that huge, loving family, along with my father. But
something always stops me," she confessed, her
voice thick with misery.

He was silent for a moment. "Now's not the time
to figure out why," he said finally. "The best we can
do for now is to distract you." Warm, strong hands
dropped to her shoulders, turning her around to face
his eyes. For once he looked neither distant nor aloof,
and the smile that curved his mouth was gentle. "I've
never kissed a nun before," he murmured, touching
her lips briefly with his. "It should be quite illuminating."

And then he pulled her the rest of the way into his
arms, cradling her against his solid warmth, her hips
molded to his, as he kissed her, long and slow and deep.

It was about the most effective thing he could have done. She finished preparing the dinner in a daze, then sat through it dreamily, smiling at everyone, making light conversation as his hand caught hers under the table. She even survived Elinor's enthusiastic exclamations during the tour of the apartment with sunny grace, her romantic haze keeping her oblivious to the curious glances James kept alternating between her and Elinor.

Would she go to bed with him that night? she wondered as she curled up in one of the overstuffed chairs, her feet tucked up underneath her as she sipped her espresso. The conversation flowed around her, and every now and then she'd murmur something appropriate as she allowed herself the luxury of watching him out of heavy-lidded eyes. Should she sleep with him or kick him out with Charles and Elinor? Two years of celibacy shouldn't be ended lightly. But it would undoubtedly be ended gloriously. Even his drawled voice set her nerve ends on fire.

But perhaps that was the greater danger. James Elliott wouldn't be dismissed as lightly as Sebastian Coddaire, or any of Lucia's brief affairs. As a matter of fact, it was more than likely that he would be the one to do the dismissing, and not her at all. And could she bear it if he did? Wouldn't it be better to keep her distance early on? James Elliott could far too easily shatter everything she'd worked for in her life.

But looking at those long, slim hands as they cradled the demitasse cup, she knew that for the first time in years she was going to abdicate her responsibility to herself. She would leave it up to him—it would be his decision and his blame when it all fell into ashes about them.

"You're looking quite pensive, Molly," Elinor ventured hesitantly, and determinedly Molly roused herself from her abstraction.

"Am I?" she said lightly. "I suppose I'm just tired. I haven't been sleeping well this week."

"Just this week?" James queried, amusement in his eyes.

In for a penny, in for a pound, Molly thought with sudden defiance. He'd draw his own conclusions anyway. "Actually, I don't think I've had a decent night's sleep since Jeremy Cabello's opening at the Feinham," she said frankly.

"Why, Molly, bless your heart!" A brilliant smile lit his dark face.

"On that note we'd better leave," Charles announced, getting to his feet and reaching out a solicitous hand to Elinor. "You need to catch up on your beauty sleep, my girl. We can't have you looking washed out at the wedding. People might think I never taught my daughter how to take proper care of herself."

"Don't be absurd, Charlie," Elinor chided him lightly. "Molly will look beautiful no matter what." She hesitated a moment, then went up to Molly and gave her a gentle hug. "Thank you for everything, Molly."

Molly had to steal herself not to return the embrace. The smile felt stiff on her face. "My pleasure, Elinor. And let me know if there's anything I can do for the wedding."

"Just be there." The words weren't the platitude they sounded, Molly realized. Elinor was afraid she really wouldn't come.

"Don't worry. I'll be there with bells on," she promised with a rush of warmth, and Elinor's plump shoulders relaxed slightly.

And then suddenly James was there, pulling her startled body into his arms to give her a platonic hug. "Good girl," he whispered in her ear. Aloud, he said, "I'd better be getting home too. You *do* need your sleep, Molly."

Her hands clung helplessly to his shoulders for a moment, then released him as she composed her expression. "Thanks for coming," she said with deceptive calm. "And for the flowers and all your help." *Don't leave me,* she begged silently, but for once his mind-reading ability seemed to have deserted him.

The leave-taking stretched and dragged, as leave-takings do, and it was a full five minutes later that the door finally closed behind them. Molly leaned her head against the panel, closing her eyes as a wave of longing washed over her. "Damn," she said quietly.

And then, ignoring the dishes and coffee cups and the mess, she flicked off the lights and wandered like a sleepwalker to her bedroom, dropping her clothes along the way. And despite her frustrated misgivings, sleep claimed her almost immediately. If her dreams left her even more feverish by the morning, so that she faced the mess with a moan of despair, then she had no one but herself to blame. And James Damn-him Elliott.

Chapter Thirteen

"Are you serious?" Molly breathed in amazement. The buzz of conversation around her went unheeded, and the champagne glass in her hand trembled slightly. "You can't be; you're just teasing me."

"Would I do that?" James queried smoothly, taking an unconcerned sip from his glass. It was one of the finer California vintages. One of Dr. Matheson's strictures was that, while they shouldn't skimp, California products should be used whenever possible. Therefore, California champagne was served at exhibit openings, California fruit and vegetables made up the hors d'oeuvres, and California money was enticed by these festivities into the museum endowment fund. Molly had long ago thanked providence that she loved champagne—she had had more than enough time to acquire a strong dislike of it.

The occasion of this current champagne fete was the opening of a costume exhibit, organized by a triumphant Lucia, entitled "Clothes Make the Woman." Molly had no choice but to attend, both for Lucia's sake and by Matheson's strictest orders. She had known with a sinking certainty that she would run into the one person she had studiously avoided the last few days. Though, after the first twenty-four hours, he hadn't made much of an effort, Molly realized with a chagrin that she called relief.

And indeed, she hadn't been there for ten minutes, wandering past the silver-and-gold mannequins with their eighteenth-, nineteenth-, and twentieth-century costumes, when James Elliott materialized in front of her like a rabbit out of a hat. She was standing in front of an Edwardian lace dress, eyeing it with a wistful covetousness, when he startled her by appearing by her side. His first words startled her even more.

"Mr. Seaquist wants to meet you."

Molly still couldn't quite believe him. "You must be kidding. J. E. Seaquist hasn't met anyone from the outside world in over twenty years. He's even more of a recluse than Howard Hughes was."

James smiled serenely, taking another sip of champagne. He was looking absolutely devastating, of course—Molly had yet to meet a man who looked as good in a tuxedo. Sebastian had only succeeded in looking like a high-class bouncer at a fancy restaurant, and her tame eunuchs paled into insignificance next to Elliott's splendor. "You shouldn't believe everything you read in the supermarket, darling Molly. J. E. Seaquist has been a recluse for no more than five years, and he has an excellent reason for it. His health."

"Sure."

A trace of irritation shadowed his eyes and then disappeared. "I don't know why I bother arguing with you—you can find out soon enough just how sick he is. I've told him we'll come this weekend."

"We?" she echoed suspiciously, still doubting him seriously.

"Do you think I'd abandon that helpless old man to your tender mercies? Come now, I'm not that cruel. I'll be along to protect him, and to serve as a buffer. He isn't used to meeting new people at this point, though I can assure you there have been any number of visitors to Sea Tor during the last few years. But both he and you would be more comfortable if I brought you. Any objections? Surely you're not afraid to spend the weekend with me." His voice was cool and unconcerned, and Molly could hardly come up with the thousand and one qualms that arose in her mind. Triumphantly she presented the best one.

"You know as well as I do that I can't possibly do it this weekend. Have you forgotten that my father is getting married on Saturday?"

"I'm hardly likely to forget, since I've been invited. Their wedding is set for five o'clock in the afternoon. We can drive up to Sea Tor on Friday, spend the night, and return to San Francisco by way of Madison for the wedding the next day. It's only forty miles away from Sea Tor—barely out of our way. And it gives you a perfect excuse to avoid the rehearsal dinner and all the attendant festivities." His voice was cynical.

"And why should I want to miss all that?" she queried coolly.

"You know as well as I do that you're attending the

wedding itself under duress. This way you can do your familial duty with the least trauma involved. I've already spoken to Charles and told him of our plans, and he has no great objections."

She stared at him in astonishment, and with his usual deftness he exchanged his empty champagne glass for her barely touched one. "Close your mouth, darling, you'll catch flies. Not that there would be any flies in the great Museum of American Arts. Anything with life in it would be smothered to death in minutes."

"What the hell are you talking about?" She shut her mouth with a snap.

"This museum is dead. All museums I've ever been in are dead—mummified belongings put on lifeless display for zombies to file past like docile sheep."

Everything else fled from Molly's mind for the moment. "And I suppose you think it's better for some rich old hermit to hoard away works of art like a secret perversion, gloating over them in privacy, depriving the world of great treasures that should belong to the people?"

"Art should be touched and used, not walled away in a great mausoleum."

"I'm sure Lucia will be gratified to hear your opinion of her exhibit. She slaved over this for months— she'll be thrilled to have it dismissed as a lifeless display in a mausoleum."

"I wouldn't dream of saying such a thing to her, and neither will you." The threat was implicit in his voice. "As a matter of fact, this is much better than

Matheson's usual crap. But I still contend that these clothes should be worn, by real flesh and blood human beings."

"Don't be ridiculous—the fabrics are impossibly fragile. They shred if anyone puts even a slightly rough hand on them." Her voice was outraged.

"Perhaps. But if I were a dressmaker, I'd rather my clothes shredded on a living human being than clothe lifeless dummies throughout eternity. What are you going to do with that quilt you're making? Sleep under it, use it for warmth like a normal human being? Or are you going to hang it on a wall?" he added in disgust.

"I'm going to cut it into tiny pieces and shove it down your throat until it chokes you!" she shot back viciously.

To her amazement his face lightened, and a rueful laugh broke the tension. "Bless you, Molly, I've missed you. As soon as you finish the damn quilt I'll drag you underneath it and make wild, passionate love to you." The words were spoken so softly, none of the crowd around them could hear, but her face flushed crimson nonetheless.

"Stop it, James," she said irritably. "You're the only human being I know who can make me blush."

"I'm glad to know I have that much power over you. I'll pick you up after work on Friday. It's about a three-hour drive to Sea Tor, and if we leave by five, we should arrive just in time for dinner."

She looked up at him, trying to read his face, but to no avail. Finally, she allowed her vulnerability full reign. "James," she murmured, "should I?"

"Of course you should. How many people get an invitation from J. E. Seaquist?" he said easily.

"You're right, of course."

"I usually am." He turned his attention back to the Edwardian lace dress. "Is this part of the museum's collection?" he queried with a casualness that immediately set alarm bells ringing in Molly's head.

"I believe so. Everything is except for the pink Worth dress and the Gernreich. Why? Thinking of buying it?" she demanded.

"It's a thought. You'd look absolutely magnificent in it, Molly Bloom. Like a fallen angel."

Having had the same thought herself a few moments ago, Molly felt a treacherous warmth. "Don't be absurd; I'd never fit into it," she said crossly.

"Of course you would. Quite deliciously, as a matter of fact," he murmured. "You wouldn't even need a corset like the poor lady who originally owned it must have. Not that a corset might not be a nice touch. I can see you now, all French lace and black garters."

"James!" Molly was startled into a shocked giggle. "I'm leaving you."

"You always are," he said mournfully. "Will you be there when I come to get you Friday afternoon?"

She hesitated, knowing full well she should refuse, knowing full well she should continue to keep as far away from him as possible. Each day had got a little bit easier, until the memories came flooding back with his reappearance. If she had any sense at all, she should tell him no.

"Yes," she said. And with a smug smile and a nod

he left her, wandering back through the crowd with his usual grace, leaving Molly to stare after him with longing eyes. And then she realized he had deftly changed the subject before she could find out when he'd spoken with her father. The idea of the two of them getting together to talk about her was distinctly unsettling, and she considered striking out after James, through the sea of beautiful people that thronged the exhibit. But, no, that could wait until Friday.

And as for her decision, she thought, turning back to the Edwardian mannequin with a dressmaker's eye, well, it was for the sake of Seaquist, wasn't it? What sane human being would turn down a chance like that? The fact that James Elliott came along with the deal was just an unfortunate coincidence that she'd have to put up with. A small, wistful smile lit her face at the thought of putting up with James Elliott, and she went in search of more champagne.

She was ready and waiting for him when he appeared at her door at five minutes to five on Friday afternoon. She had chosen her apparel carefully: a pair of faded venerable jeans hugged her generous curves, the aqua-green silk shirt could be opened to an enticing level if she felt the urge, and the thick gray sweater would cover a multitude of sins. Her freshly washed blond hair hung in a thick curtain around her slightly defiant face, and her boots were old and beautiful ones Charles had brought back from Spain several years ago.

If she'd hoped to irritate James with her casual attire, she was doomed to disappointment. There was a distinctly predatory look in his eyes as they traveled over her lush curves, but he contented himself with a noncommittal greeting.

"You're ready," he observed. "I like that. Not that you wouldn't be worth waiting for, but I'm just as glad I don't have to."

"Damn," she said silkily, drawing on a herring-bone-tweed riding jacket.

"Damn?" he echoed, picking up her overnight case.

"If I'd only known I could have managed to dawdle a good hour and a half..." she said in her sweetest voice.

"It's going to be like that, is it?" he said warily. "Let me assure you, Molly Bloom, you would *not* have dawdled an hour and a half. I'd give you fifteen minutes, longer than I'd give anyone else, and then I'd carry you downstairs in whatever state of undress you happened to be in."

"Carry me?" she scoffed. "That I'd like to see. I'm a bit more of an armful than you seem to realize."

"And I'm a bit more of a man than you realize," he shot back quite simply. There was no overweening masculine bravado in his voice—it was a simple statement of fact, and Molly was inclined to believe him. "Never mind, Molly. You'll find that out in good time."

"I don't like the sound of that."

"Don't you?" He paused in the doorway, and the distant expression vanished from his face for a moment, leaving him curiously vulnerable. "Do you trust me?"

"Hardly!" she scoffed, ignoring the treacherous weakening of her resolve.

He set the suitcase down, the expression on his face almost frighteningly stern. "Then you'd better not come with me," he said flatly. "At your age you should know better than to go off with a man you can't trust."

She considered calling his bluff, then decided against it. "Why do you think I surround myself with tame eunuchs?" she questioned lightly. "They're completely safe."

"I'm sure they are," he grated. "Would you rather stay home with them?"

"I'm here and dressed, aren't I?" Her husky voice was irritable to cover any indecision. "And on time, for that matter, which I'll have you know is a fairly rare occurrence for me. Are *you* having second thoughts? Afraid I'm going to tell your boss just how unethical you've been in acquiring pieces for his precious collection?"

"No," he said, moving across the room to her. "No, I'm not having second thoughts, and, no, I'm not afraid you'll expose my so-called nefarious dealings. I'm just not sure if I like being with someone who thinks me capable of— What is it you think I'm capable of, for that matter?"

She eyed him warily. "Oh, I think you're capable of just about anything if you thought it was justified."

"You do wonders for my ego," he said dryly. "Are you afraid I'm going to take you to bed this weekend? Destroy your precious celibacy?"

No, I'm afraid you won't, she thought, and then was

panicked both by the thought and the latent fear that she'd spoken that thought out loud.

James still had that uncanny ability to read her mind. "Or are you afraid that I won't?" he paraphrased softly, his eyes devouring her intently.

"Don't be ridiculous," she scoffed, so effectively she half-believed it herself. "I'm not afraid of anything you might or might not try, James Elliott. I'm more than a match for you."

"That's what I've been trying to tell you," he said smoothly, barely hidden amusement restoring his equanimity. "Come on, vixen. We're running late." Catching up her heavy suitcase, he strode out the door with his usual feline grace, not even bothering to check whether she was following, Molly realized in disgust.

And without further hesitation she trailed him out the door, dreaming of revenge.

Chapter Fourteen

She dressed carefully for dinner that night, telling herself that all her care was to ensure she made a good impression on one of the twenty richest men in the world, telling herself that her damp palms, pounding heart, and intense concentration on looking as beautiful as she could was simply due to an interest in J. E. Seaquist and his extensive art collection, not the infuriating James Elliott.

Really, there was nothing left to do, and here it was, fifteen minutes before the appointed dinner hour. The new dress had been an inspired choice. The black silk molded gracefully to her ripe curves, swirled around her long legs, and hugged her full breasts. She had been sparing with her makeup—a light hand with the blusher to emphasize her cheekbones, and mascara and eye pencil that did wonders for her usually laughing blue eyes, giving them a sultry look. The blond hair hung in a mane of artfully tangled curls, but no artifice could explain her shining eyes and curiously vulnerable mouth.

It had been a surprisingly amiable drive up to Sea

Tor, despite their bickering beginning. James seemed determined to stick to neutral subjects, entertaining Molly with a fascinating account of Seaquist's early years on Wall Street, when robber barons were the rule rather than the exception. There was a feeling of easy camaraderie that lasted through their arrival at the Seaquist estate, perched high above the Pacific Ocean, until once more Molly's misgivings had risen.

And all for nothing. A motherly-looking house-keeper had immediately shown her up to the magnificent bedroom she now paced, complete with silk draperies, a Watteau on the wall, an Aubusson beneath her feet, the delicate furniture old enough to have miraculously survived the ravages of the French Revolution. The bed was on a raised platform, draped in silk, and it looked as if it once held Madame Pompadour and all her lovers.

The knowledge that James Elliott was comfortably ensconced in his own room in another wing of the rambling building and presumably had no intention of sharing that sybaritic-looking bed set the seal on her relief, a relief that looked oddly like disappointment in her expressive eyes.

"You're ready?" James's smooth voice broke through her abstraction, and she turned from her stance by the balcony overlooking the formal gardens with their plundered Greek and Roman statuary.

"Don't you knock?" she questioned irritably.

"Only when I have to," he replied, his glittering eyes sweeping over her with approval. "What have you been doing, counting up the foreign statuary? I suppose you think it shouldn't be here either. I assure you it was long gone from its country of origin when J. E. bought it."

"That doesn't mean it can't still be returned," she snapped back. Only if she stayed angry could she fight the insidious attraction James held for her. The more she saw him, the more she wanted him. And the more she wanted him, the more she was determined to resist.

"Stop looking for problems, Molly," he said with his usual uncanny perception. "We have quite enough to work out between us as it is. Do you like your room?"

"Very nice," she said briefly, dismissing the glorious elegance that had left her in awed wonder her first few minutes alone in the bedroom. "I was delighted to hear you've been put in the west wing. I trust there are long passageways and securely locked doors?"

An ironic smile lit his face. "Molly, do you seriously think a few locked doors and staircases would stand in my way if I wanted you? You're the only inhabitant of the east wing. My...employer has rooms on the first floor, and the servants have separate quarters. So there's nothing to stop me from creeping into your bedroom in the dark of night and having my wicked way with you, if I so desire."

"Nothing but your own good sense," she shot back, the horrible phrase *if I wanted you* echoing in her mind. "Isn't Mr. Seaquist waiting for us?"

"He's running a little late." A troubled expression momentarily darkened his face. "He's gone downhill since I've seen him. Try not to be too surprised if he seems pretty weak. He's a sick man, and he's eighty-seven years old. But you don't need to worry. As his body fails, his mind seems to get sharper. You'll like him, Molly. And he'll like you."

"Does it matter?" she queried abruptly, and he gave her a long, considering look.

"It matters to me, yes," he said obscurely, taking her arm in a light grip that nevertheless seemed to burn through the thin material of her dress. "No more questions, Molly Bloom. Come along."

The legendary J. E. Seaquist was a far cry from what she had expected. A thin, frail old man, his face seamed and lined with age and pain, he sat huddled in a wheelchair, a plaid blanket wrapped around his shoulders, a solicitous, matronly nurse by his side. Molly's steps had faltered as James led her into the fire-warmed blue-and-green lounge, reluctant to impose on such an obviously aged and infirm old man, when his sunken head lifted, and his blue eyes, faded but still full of life, met hers, and a smile wreathed his weary face.

"James, you were right," he exclaimed softly. "A Renaissance lady if ever I've seen one. A Florence madonna, do you think?"

"Absolutely not, J. E.," James said easily, leading her bewitched figure over to the seated man. "I see her as the image of a Venetian courtesan. All that gold hair and ripe flesh."

"Watch it, you two," Molly said sharply. "If I hear the word Rubens, you'll be in deep trouble."

"Never, my dear, absolutely never," Seaquist promised solemnly, a light in those faded eyes. "Come here and kiss a tired old man. I never have any pretty young ladies to kiss me anymore, and I claim the privilege."

Gracefully Molly leaned over and kissed the papery cheek, sitting on a stool beside him as he caught hold of her hand in his thin, clawlike one.

"Now, Mr. Seaquist, what will the young lady think of such lies?" the nurse demanded cheerfully. "You have me and Mrs. Baldwin to keep you well-supplied with kisses."

"That I do, Peg," he shot back. "But I like a bit of variety now and then."

"You're as incorrigible as ever, J. E.," James said from his position by the bar.

"Of course I am. Age only makes me more outrageous." The old man winked at Molly, and she smiled back. "I'll have a damnably weak and watery Scotch on the rocks, my boy. After you take care of the ladies, that is."

"Since when have you been allowed to drink again?" James demanded.

"Since the doctors decided they couldn't do anything for me and I might as well be allowed to go out in peace," he snapped back, nettled. James turned a stricken glance to the nurse, and she nodded her head in grim agreement.

"All right, J. E.," he said finally. "I always thought you were too tough to let a little thing like Scotch have much effect on you anyway. What would you like, Molly?"

"Damnably weak and watery Scotch on the rocks also. Unless you think I'm not tough enough to take it?" she questioned mischievously.

"Oh, I think you're tough enough. Between you and J. E., I'd be hard put to pick the meaner, more ornery, pigheaded..."

"You have quite some relationship with that young man, don't you?" Seaquist cackled approvingly. "I've never seen him so taken with a female. Usually he just showers flowery compliments on them that don't mean a damn thing. You can tell he likes you when he calls you names."

"And you have quite a relationship with him yourself," she replied. "Do you let all your employees talk to you that way?"

"Hell, James is more than just an employee. He's—" A hasty movement from James broke the old man's sentence in midstream. "He's a family friend," he finished smoothly.

"Now, why do I think that wasn't what you were about to say?" Molly questioned sweetly.

Another cackle escaped the old man. "She is sharp, James. You told me she was, and I should have believed you. I should have known it would take more than a pretty face to win you. Tell me, Molly, how did you get interested in American art, and how do you like working for Matheson? He used to work for me a great many years ago, and I always found him a brilliant but difficult young man. Rather like my—like James there."

Handing pale amber drinks all around, James cast a quelling glance at his employer. "I fail to see any resemblance."

"But I do." Molly laughed delightedly, taking a cautious sip of her weak drink. "You're just like Dr.

Matheson when he's in one of his irascible genius moods.''

"Still puts on those acts, does he?" Seaquist questioned with interest. "I hope he realizes what a treasure he's got in you."

"How would you know what a treasure he's got in me, sir?" Molly questioned cheerfully.

"I have my sources, a slightly biased James among them. Tell me more about your tenure at the Museum of American Arts. I've missed a lot being cooped up in this place."

The next two and a half hours were a real workout for Molly, intellectually, professionally, and emotionally. Seaquist seemed intent on learning everything he could know about her professional background, her education, what had drawn her to museum work, her various areas of interest. He was as knowledgeable an inquisitor as she was a respondent, and she barely noticed her meal or James's amused expression as he watched her in silence. It wasn't until the china-and-ormolu eighteenth-century French clock struck eleven that she roused herself enough to realize that she had just gone through an almost grueling inquisition.

"I suppose you're going to insist on dragging me to bed, Peg?" he demanded querulously of his nurse. "Any chance I could talk you into another half hour?"

"Not tonight, Mr. Seaquist," she said sternly. "You've had more than enough stimulation for one day. Mr. Elliott and Dr. McDonough will be here tomorrow—you can continue your talks over breakfast."

"More likely brunch, if I know you, J. E.," James said easily. "He's taken to sleeping sinfully late, Molly. Turning into a night owl, aren't you, J. E.? We'll meet you at eleven for coffee and croissants."

"Fine for you—I want bacon and eggs. And I'm allowed to have them again, not those damn awful substitutes. What do you think of that?" he demanded defiantly.

"I think, in that case, that I'll join you for bacon and eggs," James said mildly enough, refusing to be drawn. "Sleep well, J. E."

"Don't count on it. Give me a kiss good night, girl," he ordered an obedient Molly. "You'll have bacon and eggs with James and me, won't you?"

"You bet." His hand trembled slightly in hers, and the purple-blue shadows of exhaustion had appeared below his sunken, crepey eyes. "Good night, Mr. Seaquist."

"Call me J. E., girl. After all, you're almost one of the family." And on that final, cryptic utterance, he allowed Peg to wheel him from the room.

Molly met James's eyes across the table. "He's very dear, isn't he?" she questioned softly.

"He is. He doesn't sleep much at night anymore—he only manages to drift off for an hour or two before the pain wakes him up again," he said flatly.

Molly swallowed a lump in her throat. "He doesn't have long, does he?"

"No." James's voice was rough. "But he's had a good long life, and he doesn't have any complaints."

She hesitated a moment, then finally voiced the question that had plagued her. "Perhaps you could explain something to me. Why did I get the feeling that this evening was a rather entertaining job interview? All the little details of my career would hardly interest even the most bored old man if he didn't have some ulterior motive."

"Are you hoping he's going to fire me and put you in my place? Don't hold your breath, Molly darling."

"Then it was my imagination?"

He hesitated, pushing back his chair and walking around the table to her side. "I wouldn't say that either," he murmured, pulling her chair out for her. "But it's none of my business. Why don't we go for a walk in the gardens. There's something I've been wanting to show you—if you can control your puritan tendencies long enough to enjoy it without demanding that it be sent back to Italy."

"I'll try" was all she could promise as she allowed him to lead her out onto the terrace. His hand was lightly possessive on the small of her back, and sternly she ordered herself to ignore it. *Forget Seaquist's mistaken notion that you mean anything to his fair-haired boy. Forget the fact that the very thought of James Elliott drives celibacy completely out of your mind, not to mention his touch, his smell, his feel. Remember that damning phrase "if I wanted you," and the fact that if James Elliott broke your heart, he'd do a far more catastrophic job than Sebastian Coddaire could even dream of. For heaven's sake, Molly, watch your step.*

But the night air was out to sabotage her. Record-high temperatures had been reported all over the northern half of the state, and right now it felt more like June than early November. Unlike their chilly picnic some three weeks earlier, Molly was perfectly comfortable without a sweater, clad only in her light dress, and the soft, damp sea breeze teased her nostrils and seduced her senses. She could hear the crash of the sea on the rocks below Sea Tor, and unconsciously she sighed.

"Very romantic, isn't it?" James read her mind again, his voice noncommittal as he led her down a terraced garden and through a thick hedge.

"I suppose so," she replied distantly. "How far is it to the cliffs and the ocean?"

"Not far. See that white gazebo to the left? That's the closest lookout point. If you want, we can wander over that way afterward."

"That might be nice," she said politely. "I wouldn't want to put you to any trouble."

A small, secret smile lit his face. "Oh, no trouble at all, Dr. McDonough," he said with equal formality.

Molly's hand clenched into a fist, then slowly she let out a dispirited sigh. "God, you are so frustrating," she swore. "I never know how to take you."

"I've warned you before I don't fit into your tidy little categories," he said calmly, removing his hand from the small of her back and taking her hand in his. It disappeared in his larger one, and the feel of the lightly calloused skin against her soft palm brought back all sorts of unbearably erotic memories. She considered yanking her hand away, then dismissed the idea as childish. Besides, it felt too good to deny herself that comfort and pleasure. And it was becoming more than apparent that seduction was the last thing on his mind this weekend.

"Shall I confess something rather embarrassing?" she said shyly, the darkness covering them with a beneficial velvety warmth. "Before I met J. E., I thought he might be my father."

James's hand gripped hers suddenly, then loosened. "What in the world made you think that?" His voice was deliberately light, but Molly thought she could recognize some tension there.

"I don't know. I just thought it was pretty strange that such a famous recluse would be willing to meet me, and for no particular reason. I have a strongly romantic streak, you know. I used to pretend that the queen of England was my mother and Gregory Peck was my father."

A low laugh escaped him. "That's a hell of a combination."

"Oh, I didn't think of them both at the same time. I'd take turns with my fantasies, depending on which parent I was mad at at the time." She shook her head ruefully. "Do you realize that most nonadopted children have the same fantasies?"

"Of course. I used to wish that Davy Crockett was my real father," James said easily. "So what makes you think that J. E. isn't your long-lost father?"

"I knew it the moment I met him," she said simply. "It wasn't anything intellectual—it was emotional. I took one look and knew he wasn't any kin to me."

"Were you disappointed?"

"Not really. Charles is more than enough father for me," she replied. "I was just curious."

"And do you think you would know your birth parents if you were to meet them? Some magic lightbulb would turn on in your head or something?''

"I don't know. I think I'd feel something. Whether I'd recognize them or not, I couldn't say. But it wouldn't be just the pleasant fondness I felt for J. E.''

"Well, I'm just as glad you're not J. E.'s natural daughter," he said solemnly.

"Why?"

"Because then you'd be heir to his art collection and his fortune instead of nine mainly disinterested nieces and nephews, and I know you'd delight in holding all that power over my head.''

"It's a lovely thought," she said cheerfully. "But why do I have the idea that wasn't what you really were about to say?''

"Because you're paranoid," he replied. "Here it is.''

They had turned a corner among the tall shrubbery, and standing in front of them, silvered in the moonlight, was a bronze statue. "Oh, James," she breathed, releasing his hand and moving forward in wonder. "It's a Scarpiello, isn't it?''

"It is. One of his lesser-known pieces, commissioned for an American millionaire in the 1850's. *The Lovers,* it's called, for obvious reasons. J. E. adores it.''

"I don't blame him," she said softly. "They're very beautiful. It looks as if she'll come to life beneath his hands.''

"You would think so, wouldn't you?" James said meditatively, walking around the bronze statue with an impartial eye. The two bronze lovers were inextricably intertwined, molded throughout eternity in each others' arms. Their position set off a train of erotic thought in Molly's mind that she did her best to banish. "I think she looks like you," he added, further upsetting her equilibrium. "The way you come alive under my hands."

Molly's knees felt curiously weak with longing at his words. "Damn you, James," she said dizzily, "she does not." But she did, her bronze hair rippling down her back as her head was thrown back in pleasure. She could very well have posed for it more than a century ago.

"Of course she does. Why else do you think I bought her?" he said silkily.

"*You* bought her?" Molly was startled into facing him, and the sight of his tall, dangerous body on the other side of the statue further weakened her resolve. "I assumed she'd been here since the place was built."

"Hardly. J. E.'s wife would never have allowed it—she was a dear heart but very prudish. No, I bought it a month ago, not long after our meeting at the Feinham Gallery. I couldn't get over the resemblance."

"I'm surprised you don't have it in your bedroom too," she snapped weakly.

"I thought of it, but the floor isn't strong enough to withstand the weight. She's a pretty hefty creature, she and her lover."

Molly allowed herself a mild glare, holding her ground as James began to circle the statue back to her side. *He's going to kiss me,* she thought somewhat daz-

edly. *He's going to take me in his arms and draw me
down onto the grass in front of the statue and make long,
sweet, soul-destroying love to me, and I won't fight him
anymore.*

She waited, her eyes glowing, her lips parted, until
he reached her side. "Shall we go back?" he said
calmly.

She stared at him for a long silent moment. And
then, without a word, she turned and ran from him,
across the lawn in her high-heeled sandals, not stopping for breath until she was in her room, the door
slammed and locked behind her. When her heart had
finally thudded back to a semblance of normalcy, she
left the door to wander weakly into the room, wondering what on earth had possessed her to run from him
like that. Walking over to the small balcony, she
looked out over the moonlit garden to the gazebo on
the edge of the sea, and saw the solitary male figure
standing there, staring out at the ocean.

Chapter Fifteen

Molly came suddenly, startlingly awake, and the womblike depths of the darkened room sent her sleep-dazed brain into a temporary panic until memory returned, along with the bright moonlight illuminating the gracious proportions of the room and the bed that had provided her with such a restless night's sleep.

Not that it was the fault of the bed, Molly thought wearily, dragging her tired body out from under the light covers and onto the cool marble floor. It was James Elliott, or, more correctly, the lack thereof, that was playing havoc with her sleep patterns. The tiny travel clock beside her bed said three thirty, and Molly knew without a doubt that that was all the sleep she could count on for now, with her body burning with a feverish longing, and that all-too-familiar clutching feeling in the pit of her stomach.

She had never felt this way with Sebastian, this overwhelming, soul-shattering need. She had never felt this way with anyone. But the very idea of James Elliott filtered through her thoughts, her dreams, until she was a sleep-haunted wreck, while he, no doubt, slept the sleep of the just, she thought wryly.

Well, she had never been one to suffer in silence, or to give up without a struggle. A nice moonlit walk to the sea would help, on probably the last warm night of the year, and a detour on the way back via the lounge and the brandy decanter would also prove efficacious. And tomorrow she would be just as cool and unruffled as her nemesis. Never again would she allow her longing for him to override her good judgment.

There was a very simple cure for all this, she decided, tying the thin silk wrapper around the clinging peau de soie nightgown she had inexplicably spent a small fortune on just two days ago. She would pick one of her tame eunuchs, all of whom had been more than eager for her favors, and go to bed with him. Someone handsome, she decided, her bare feet silent on the curving marble staircase. Even better, someone exquisitely beautiful, like Julian Benson or Kent Devereaux, who would both put James's rather predictable charms into the shade, she thought maliciously.

Except that Julian was still in love with his wife, and was a bore in the bargain, and Kent, though more entertaining, was still desperately in love with his reflection. Sleeping with Sebastian would be a perfect alternative, bound to turn James livid with rage, but Molly doubted she was capable of going that far. Besides, this was supposed to be distraction and cure, not revenge. Wasn't it?

The soft ocean breeze caressed her skin as she

wandered barefoot over the moonlit grass toward the gazebo. It was slightly cooler than it had been a few hours earlier, and belatedly she wished she'd brought a blanket to wrap around her while she sat and watched the sea. Well, her time would simply have to be cut short if the breeze proved too intense. Perhaps the railing around the gazebo would provide a modicum of shelter from the wind.

There were a few dead leaves underfoot as she mounted the short flight of steps up to the octagonal building. All the furniture had been removed, probably in advance of the cooler weather, but a seat ran around the railing, and Molly perched there, looking out at the ink-dark ocean, her arms clasped tightly around her knees, her bare feet tucked up beneath the silken folds of her nightdress and wrapper, as she contemplated the current mess her life was in.

"Aren't you cold?" His voice, low and beguiling, floated over to her, and she wondered briefly at her lack of surprise. Slowly she turned her head, to see him silhouetted against the entrance to the gazebo, clad only in a faded pair of jeans and a shirt open around his dark smooth chest. It flapped slightly in the breeze, putting Molly in mind of a mysterious white bird.

She shook her head in answer to his question, not trusting her voice, and turned back to stare out at the midnight-blue ocean. She could feel him move closer, though the sound of his bare feet on the wooden floor of the gazebo was indiscernible. She knew that all she had to do was lean back and his tall, strong body would support her, his lean warmth sinking into her bones. Determinedly she kept her body upright and her eyes straight ahead.

"Why did you run?" he asked with what sounded like idle curiosity.

"Why do I always run?" she replied, throwing caution to the wind-tossed sea.

"You usually run when I'm trying to seduce you. This time you seemed to run because I wasn't."

"I guess there's no pleasing me." She shrugged with an attempt at indifference.

"I wouldn't say that," he drawled, and the inherent promise in his voice sent shivers down her spine.

Steeling herself, she turned to meet his gaze, then wished she hadn't. The intensity in the gray depths seemed to see right through her weak defenses, and she realized with a sudden start that he had accomplished just what he had so obviously set out to do. He had demoralized her, seduced her, turned her into a desperate, weak-willed, lovelorn creature who hungered for his touch; turned her into someone who thought celibacy and independence a poor second to love. And she hated him for it, almost as much as she wanted him.

And now that he had accomplished his objective, the prize seemed to have lost its interest for him. "What is it you want from me, James?" she said suddenly, her husky voice soft on the night air.

A small smile lit his face. "Have I confused you that much, Molly?" A hand reached out and tenderly pushed a strand of hair behind her ear. "I thought it was very clear. I want you. In my arms. In my bed."

"For how long?"

"Until we tire of one another," he said lightly. "Surely you wouldn't want me to promise some garbage about happily ever after? We're both too realistic for that."

"Of course," Molly said, lying in her teeth. Slowly she rose, standing in front of him, her silken gown trailing about her feet, her hair a curtain down her back, not knowing how very vulnerable and very beautiful she was to James's hungry eyes. "Aren't you going to make love to me?" she questioned calmly. "I won't fight you anymore."

Slowly he shook his head. "No, I'm not." Instead, he took a deliberate step away from her, and the withdrawal of his body heat was an aching loss.

"Why not?" There was no keeping the mournful note out of her voice. "Do you get some kick out of teasing me?"

A hint of a smile played over his mouth. "Just a little bit," he admitted shamelessly. "You respond so beautifully. But I also told myself that I wasn't going to seduce you against your will, that I wasn't going to overpower your misgivings and let you tell yourself it's my fault. If you want to go to bed with me, you have to decide. You have to tell me and show me."

"You demand a lot, don't you?" she said quietly, watching him out of unreadable blue eyes. "Not just victory, but a complete rout."

"I don't see it in terms of victory and defeat." His voice was cool and enticing to her ears, and she wondered if she had the faintest chance against his powerful attraction.

She tried one last time, a wry smile lighting her

moon-shadowed face. "And if I don't make that decision, I'm safe?" she countered. "You'll only make love to me on your terms or not at all?"

"Yes," he said firmly, and Molly let out a chicken-hearted sigh of relief.

"Thank heavens for small favors," she said with a shaky laugh, making a sudden dash past his lean, shadowy figure. "See you tomorrow, James."

He caught her by the stairway, one iron hand clasping her wrist and whirling her around so that she fell against the solid strength of his body, into the doubtful haven of his arms. His mouth caught hers, alive with a hungry passion, and without a moment's hesitation she responded, opening her mouth beneath his passionate assault, her arms somehow finding their way around his neck to pull him closer to her trembling body.

Slowly, reluctantly, he pulled his mouth away, panting slightly for breath as he stared down at her, cradled in the circle of his arms. "I lied," he said, his voice a rasp. "I'll take you any way I can get you." His lips burned a hot, hungry trail across her cheek, capturing one tender earlobe in his strong white teeth, the tiny pleasure-pain sending a shaft of aching desire shooting through her loins.

"You're terrible," she whispered silkily against his skin. "A sneaking, devious, tricky—" His mouth caught hers in the midst of her lazy recriminations for a brief, silencing moment before trailing on to her other ear. "You know as well as I do what you're doing to me, what you have been doing to me this last month."

"I know," he verified against her vulnerable throat, his breath warm and tickling against her skin. "I wasn't sure you did. You can be damnably pigheaded, Molly."

"Not anymore," she whispered, and slowly he raised his head to look down into her vulnerable eyes.

"What does that mean?"

"It means that I want you, James. I want you so much, I think I might die from it," she said, and reaching up, she pressed her soft, open lips against his, the tip of her tongue shyly tracing the hard contours of his mouth. She could feel the groan that reverberated through his body as his tongue caught hers in a brief, savage duel for control. The feel of that rough-textured intruder made her weak with longing for still another invasion, one she had been denied too long, and her trembling hands slid under his shirt, up his smoothly muscled back, her fingers glorying in the feel of his heated flesh. Her skin was afire beneath his touch, and the silk wrapper fell to the floor in a shimmering pool around their bare feet. One sure hand reached out, pushing the thin straps off her shoulders and down to her waist, to expose the taut, straining rise of her full breasts. His beautiful hands caught them, caressed them, worshiping them with his sure touch as his thumbs rubbed lightly back and forth across the tight nipples. And then, bending his dark head down, his mouth followed, his tongue teasing the aroused flesh of first one, then the other, until Molly felt her breath come in short, uncontrollable gasps as she felt her knees give way.

Slowly, gently, he lowered her down onto the thin silk robe that lay spilled out beneath them on the floor of the gazebo, and with deft hands he pulled the rest of her nightgown down off her hips, tossing it away, his eyes never leaving her lush, moon-silvered body.

"You're so beautiful, Molly," he said reverently, shrugging out of his shirt and reaching for the waistband of his jeans. His eyes were dark and smoldering as he knelt over her. "I don't think I've ever wanted anyone or anything so much in my life."

Pulling herself into a sitting position with unconscious, primitive grace, she covered his hands with hers, moving them out of the way as her small trembling hands reached for the button of his jeans. Unable to resist, she ran lightly questing fingers over the angry bulge that strained against the tight denim, and his groan of response brought an answering tightening in her loins. On impulse she leaned forward, pressing her soft cheek against his fiery desire, her blond hair flowing over his flat stomach as her fingers slowly teased the zipper down, inch by lingering inch.

"Oh, God, Molly." His ragged cry as she finally released him from his confinement put the final touch on her readiness. Sinking back onto the wide plank floor, she looked up at him beseechingly out of passion-dark eyes.

"Please, James," she begged. "Now."

"But you're not ready," he murmured, leaning over her. "You haven't let me—"

Taking his hand, she drew it to the heart of her desire, warm and moist and welcoming. "I've been ready since that Saturday on your couch," she whispered desperately. "Please, James."

The time for teasing was past. Carefully, gently, he

parted her legs, levering forward until he rested just at the entrance of her desperate need. His mouth set his seal on hers, as slowly, surely, he drove deep into her, his massive strength filling her completely. And suddenly, before he could even begin the steady rhythm of love, her body went rigid, clenching around him convulsively as she felt herself falling through the mists. He held her tightly, soothingly, as the shudders racked her body, until finally they died away. And then he began to move, slowly at first, his body rocking against hers on the silk-covered wooden floor, filling her again and again with his warmth and power.

Molly was lost and floating, only aware of his warm body covering hers, his strength flowing inside of her, his breathing ragged in her ears, her own coming in sobbing little gasps. Slowly, unbelievably, she felt the tension begin to mount once more, until, as his hands reached under her and cradled her buttocks, drawing her up tight against him, she felt the last bit of earth leave her. She sobbed helplessly against his shoulder, her fists beating weakly against his back as she felt the storm gather force and fury.

"Come with me, Molly," he whispered hoarsely in her ear, driving against her. "Don't let me leave you behind." And as his body went rigid in her arms she felt the last barrier dissolve, and she was lost in the storm, clothed in swirling, misty darkness that enveloped them both in velvet warmth.

It was a long time before they fell back to earth, longer still before he finally moved from her, lying beside her and pulling her still-trembling body into the warm shelter of his arms. His breath was soft and teasing in her ear, the laughter in his voice gentle and loving.

"That was quite something," he murmured against her skin. "Worth waiting for, I'd say. Are you always going to be that easy to satisfy?"

Molly could feel the tears slowly drying on her cheeks, and a vague, dreaming part of her wondered when she had shed them. She wasn't one to cry easily. "I don't know," she replied in a shaky voice, leaning back into his smooth warm body.

"What do you mean, you don't know?" He raised himself up a bit, looking down at her vulnerable expression.

"I mean that's never happened before." In case he might not understand, she added "Never" in a tremulous voice.

"Never?" he echoed, amazed. At her shy nod a beautiful smile lit his face, and his kiss on her lips was soft and almost worshipful. "Let's go to bed."

A trembling laugh escaped her. "I thought we just did."

"No, my angel. We made love, but we have yet to go to bed together. I want to have you stretched out on white satin sheets and make long, slow love to you, the way your body deserves."

"Do you have white satin sheets on your bed?" she questioned lazily. "Mine are cotton."

"So are mine. We'll have to make do for tonight," he said. Wrapping the silken robe around her body, he amazed her by pulling her into his arms and standing up, holding her high against his chest with seemingly no effort at all. "Your room or mine?"

"James, put me down. You can't—" A warning swat on her bottom put an end to her protests.

"Don't argue, Molly. Just put your arms around me and relax. You've just had a strenuous experience," he murmured, slanting a wicked smile down at her.

"So have you," she replied, putting her arms around his neck and cuddling against him with a satisfied smile. She felt small and delicate and incredibly cherished, feelings she hadn't felt in a long time, if ever, and part of her wanted nothing more than to stay in his arms like this forever.

"But you forget, I've had a bit more practice in the last two years," he said wickedly, striding across the lawn. The first faint glow of sunrise was appearing in the east, casting a golden glow around them.

"You beast," she said comfortably. "What are you going to do about our clothes?"

"I'll sneak out and get them later," he said offhandedly, managing the terrace door with deceptive ease. "I have better things to do right now."

She looked at him, wide-eyed. "You do?" she echoed, a smile lurking in her warm blue eyes.

"I do. We have two years to make up for," he said, dropping a kiss on the tip of her nose.

"In that case maybe we'd better go to my room," she whispered. "I'm willing to bet my bed is bigger than yours."

"Why do you think I had the housekeeper put you there?" And he started up the wide marble staircase to the east wing, cradling her body against his.

Chapter Sixteen

As the Jeep sped along the highway in the afternoon, Molly nestled farther into the surprisingly comfortable seat. James had long ago given up any attempt to draw her into conversation, having met with nothing but monosyllables. His final question, some twenty minutes ago, had only further incited her brooding uncertainty.

"I hope it's anxiety about the wedding that's putting you in such an uncommunicative mood," he drawled finally, his clear gray eyes still trained on the relatively empty highway. "And not second thoughts about last night."

Molly hadn't been able to muster an answer, and with one last, irritated glance at her averted profile, he'd proceeded to ignore her.

She had had nothing *but* second thoughts since she woke up, alone in that wide bed sometime that afternoon. With a quiet sigh she leaned back, staring out at the countryside speeding by the car window. And even now, when she should be berating herself for her stupidity once more, why did the enticingly erotic memories of the early morning come back to torment her?

He hadn't allowed her time to catch her breath, regain some tiny thread of sanity. Kicking her door shut behind them, he'd carried her up onto the dais in the center of the room, tossing her down on the wide, sheet-rumpled bed and following her down, his mouth already tracing delicate patterns over silky flesh. She lay back among the feather pillows, her pale body glimmering against the white muslin sheets, watching him out of passion-drugged eyes as he feasted on her body. Lazily she reached out a hand, ruffling it through his raven hair, then clutched his smoothly muscled shoulders as he surprised her by rolling onto his back, bringing her with him.

With eager compliance she let him arrange her body over him, her hair flowing across his chest. With a tentative, astonished hand she reached out and touched him, her gentle stroke bringing forth an almost agonized groan of desire from the man positioned beneath her.

"Good heavens," she murmured wonderingly. "I wouldn't have thought...I mean, so soon—" She sighed in awe.

He laughed then, reaching up his hands to cradle her face and bring her down to meet his hungry, devouring mouth. "I have you to thank for it," he murmured against her soft lips. "I've wanted you too much, for too long, to be satisfied so easily. That was just an appetizer." He caught her lower lip between his strong white teeth, biting gently. "But now it's time for you to do some of the work."

She pulled away, looking down at the passion-dark

face beneath her, and a sudden, carefree smile lit her face. "Lazy," she chided, reaching between them to aid the slow, inevitable union. She watched as a look of almost unbearable ecstasy darkened his face at her slow, deliberate movements, and a small, quiet groan escaped him. Reaching up to catch her hips, he tried to hurry her, but she refused to be rushed.

"Now, now," she murmured, leaning down to kiss him lightly. "I thought I was the one who had to work for it this time."

For an answer he arched his hips up against her, driving in deep, and her fingers clenched his shoulders convulsively as she tried to maintain her composure. "Unless," she continued on a strangled gasp as he slowly withdrew, "you always have to...be... in...control..."

Once more he drove in, and a small, desperate whimper escaped her lips. "I just thought I might help," he said wickedly, reveling in the quiet shudders that were shaking her body. "I don't mind being passive," he added, his hands reaching up to lever her torso forward so that his hungry mouth could find one full breast. "If you'd rather, I won't move at all." Once more he thrust deep into her, and the whimper became a sob.

Leaning forward, she buried her face against the side of his neck. "All help gratefully accepted," she whispered against his neck, reveling in the feel of his hands sweeping down the length of her body, catching her hips and slowly setting the pace. Together they had rocked, back and forth, lost in a hot sweat of love, until...

"Penny for your thoughts," James's voice broke

through her erotic memories, and she blushed, a deep, becoming pink.

"Oh, that's what you were thinking about," he added knowingly. "I'm surprised at you, Molly Bloom. I thought you had decided it never happened."

"I wish it hadn't," she snapped immediately. "You took advantage of me."

"Crap. You know better than that, Molly," he shot back. "I'd say last night was a mutual seduction. I wouldn't have made love to you without you being a willing partner, and you know it."

"Then I guess we don't have to worry about a reoccurrence," she said recklessly. "I won't be willing again."

"Why not?" The words were gently spoken, enough to put some of Molly's anxious bravado to rest.

"Because it was a mistake."

"Why?" he persevered. "You can't convince me you didn't enjoy it—you're not that good an actress, either last night or right now. So what's the problem?"

"I—I don't want to get involved," she said finally. "My life is very comfortable as it is. I don't want to have to *need* a man so that I can't be happy by myself. I'm not ready to give up my independence. I—"

"No one was asking you to." James's voice was clipped, flat, and very angry. "I don't remember proposing last night."

His bitten-off words were a slap in the face. "I didn't say you did."

"And I don't remember suggesting we live together, or even carry on a long-term affair. As a matter of fact, I don't recall saying anything to indicate I viewed last night as anything more meaningful than a one-night stand."

If Molly hadn't been so outraged, she would have seen the hurt in his gray eyes, heard the lashings of pain in his cynical drawl. But embarrassment and fury kept her from recognizing anyone's vulnerability but her own. "Why, you rotten, nasty—"

His hand caught hers with a sudden warning grip. "No swearing," he said harshly. "I'm perfectly capable of pulling over and spanking you here and now."

"Try it," she offered in a silky rage.

"Don't tempt me."

"I didn't realize that I did anymore," she said acidly, all her earlier fears vanishing in the face of his unexpected rejection. "You know, you really should have explained it to me, James. If I'd known you were only interested in a one-night stand, I wouldn't have fought it so hard."

The gray eyes as they swept over her face were chilling in their anger. "That would have been for the best. You should know by now that it's the challenge that interests me, not necessarily the prize itself." With a rough jerk he pulled the Jeep to a stop on a suburban street, yanking out the parking brake with angry force.

Molly was beyond feeling anything—rage, hurt, or sorrow. She stared at him icily. "Why did you pull over? Were you thinking of having me walk home?"

"We're at the church," he said, his voice flat. "Or had you forgotten your father's getting married in another twenty minutes?"

"You go on ahead," she snapped. "I'll be along in a moment."

He hesitated. "Molly," he began in a gentler voice. "I don't want to fight with you. That's the last thing on my mind right now."

"Could you please go on in?" Even to her own ears she sounded desperate. "I need a minute or two by myself. Please?"

He let out an angry, frustrated sigh. "All right. But we have to talk."

"What else is there to say?"

"Plenty. But now is neither the time nor the place. I'll meet you in front of the church." Without another word he levered his tall lean body out of the Jeep.

She watched him stride across the lawn with a longing mixed with despair. He was so very beautiful and so very dangerous. She had to stop this desperate infatuation before it got any more out of hand. Already she felt enmeshed by her own desire and wretched weakness for him. And Seaquist's warmth this morning, the promise he'd wrung out of her to return to visit him, only added to the strings that bound her.

Five minutes later, cool, composed, her makeup and hair perfect, she locked the Jeep doors and walked across the thick green lawn to meet James's aristocratic figure, the keys tucked safely in her small clutch purse. The look on his handsome aloof face was studiously polite, and Molly met his inquiring glance with an equally distant nod. Taking his arm, she allowed him to lead her into the crowded church, not knowing if the sudden tightening in her stomach was due to the upcoming wedding or the man at her side.

"Why is everyone staring at me?" she whispered as they took their seats. For some inexplicable reason the usher, without asking, had placed them on the bride's side of the church, and it seemed to Molly as if every eye in the place was trained on her.

"You're being paranoid again," James said lightly, but his hand caught hers and held it tightly in a curiously comforting grip. Molly didn't pull away.

A heavily made-up matron on the shady side of sixty, dressed in blue polyester with eyelids and hair to match, was staring at her from the other side of James with undisguised curiosity. Molly could only be glad she had an aisle seat, with James's larger body to protect her from Elinor's curious friends and family. This was turning out to be far worse an ordeal than even she had expected.

Her torment hadn't even begun. The very traditional wedding march had been eschewed in favor of Bach, and slowly, gracefully, four young matrons made their way down the aisle, past Molly's horrified gaze. They were Elinor's daughters, Charles had told her, and the four of them looked enough alike to be quadruplets, despite the necessary difference in their ages. And Molly knew, to her dazed horror, that she would have made a perfect match to those four young women.

She could feel James's eyes on her rigid face. Her brain told her he was still holding her hand, quite tightly, but the nerve endings were numb, as following the four bridesmaids came Elinor's youngest granddaughter. Her face was even more familiar to Molly—she'd seen it often enough in the portrait Charles had had painted of Molly at age six.

Charles and Elinor followed, arm in arm, as the congregation surged to its feet. James tugged at her numb figure and unthinkingly she rose, following his lead, sitting when he sat, kneeling when he knelt, all the time holding on to his hand like a lifeline.

They looked so happy, so pleased with themselves, Molly thought distantly. Together at last. It was no wonder that everyone stared at her—the bastard child come home to roost.

The ceremony passed in a merciful daze. As Charles and Elinor moved joyfully back down the aisle she felt their anxious eyes on her, and then they were gone. Obediently she rose to her feet at James's pressure, looking up to meet the overwhelming concern in his face.

"Are you all right?" His voice was low and tender.

"You knew?" The words came out sounding slightly rusty.

"I guessed the first time I met Elinor. I didn't realize it was going to be so obvious, or I would have done something. Molly, I—"

Suddenly the polyester lady was pushing past them, her false teeth displayed in a large bright smile. "And which one are you, my dear? I thought I had met all of Elinor's kin in the years I've known her, but I can't quite place you. Are you her brother Bernard's child?" The avid curiosity in her crepey, blue-lidded eyes finally broke through the curtain of numbness that had enveloped Molly.

"Excuse me," she gasped, turning and pushing her way past the milling crowd. She could see James's tall figure back in the sea of people, fighting his way toward her, but luck was with her and against him. The crowds that opened so obligingly for her desperate figure closed back in front of James, obstructing him, so that Molly made it out the side exit a safe distance ahead of him.

The wedding party was arranged on the front lawn for pictures. With stumbling footsteps Molly ran past them, ignoring her father's voice as he called after her. The Jeep was farther away than she remembered, but James must have been well and truly trapped by the cheerful crowds. By the time she had screeched past the church he was still nowhere in sight. Eyes straight ahead, she headed the Jeep back toward San Francisco.

Chapter Seventeen

"Do you make a habit of running away from painful situations?"

It was past midnight. Molly had made the four-hour drive in record time, arriving at her apartment a little after nine. She had left the keys in the Jeep out in front of the building. If James was able to follow her, he could pick it up without bothering her, she had thought. If he didn't get back from the wedding until tomorrow and some enterprising thief noticed the Jeep, then so much the worse for him. She didn't care.

Stumbling into the darkened apartment, she had kicked off her thin-strapped sandals and headed for the large wing chair by her empty but functional fireplace. Ignoring her beige linen suit, she had curled up in it, staring dry-eyed and sightless into the darkened living room as the hours passed.

She didn't move a muscle at the sound of the key in the lock, didn't blink when James flicked on a light switch, flooding the room with bright light. She didn't even bother to look up at him when, slamming the door behind him, he crossed the room to tower over her.

"No answer?" he mused. "I don't suppose I really expected one. You're going to have to break some of these habits of yours, Molly," he drawled. "You can't run away from everything that hurts, you can't curl up in a tight little ball and withdraw when you don't want to answer, and you can't keep leaving me stranded without a vehicle. It's bad enough when it's your own car; when it's mine, I draw the line."

"Go away, James."

"She talks!" he marveled. "I don't suppose I dare hope that you might make an effort to communicate with me? Or are you still too busy running?"

"Leave me alone, James," she said in a dead voice. "The Jeep's parked outside and the keys are in it. Go away." She turned her face away.

"The hell I will." His voice was low and even as his hands reached out and caught Molly's upper arms in an iron grip, yanking her to her feet and shaking her until her teeth rattled. "For Christ's sake, Molly, react! Don't just stand there like a corpse, tell me what you're feeling." He shook her again, hard. "Tell me!"

Suddenly the dam of her emotions broke. "I feel betrayed!" she screamed, her control shattering into a million pieces. "I feel betrayed by all of you. By Charles and Elinor, for lying all these years. They told me my mother was dead! They lied. They tricked me and they tricked Sarah. They foisted their bastard off on her when she couldn't have a child of her own. It was no wonder she resented me—forced to put up with me all those years, the proof of her husband's infidelity.''

"Hold on a minute." His voice was sure and calm in counterpoint to her hysteria. "Where the hell did you come up with that scenario? I never realized you had such a fevered imagination."

"Damn you, don't patronize me." Breaking out of his grip, she began pounding on his chest with doubled-up fists. He stood there stolidly enough, then caught her fists in his hands, stilling their frantic attack.

"Don't jump to conclusions, Molly," he said sharply. "Charles met Elinor two years ago, a year after Sarah died. He wanted to meet your biological parents and find out what kind of people they are. Your real father died in Korea; a hero, for what it's worth. And your father found Elinor. They didn't mean to fall in love; as a matter of fact, they fought it for a long time, for your sake. But I think Charles deserves a little happiness after all these years, don't you?"

"Now who's the imaginative one?" she sneered. "You believe all that?"

"Of course I do, and so would you if you weren't so twisted by Sarah McDonough's upbringing. She's the one who made all the arrangements for the private adoption; she's the one who told you your biological parents were dead. It wasn't until Charles was going through your mother's papers after her death that he found out the truth. He should have left well enough alone, he knows that. But he was curious and at loose ends after Sarah's death. And once he met Elinor, it was too late." Slowly he released her hands. "So tell me, Molly, who betrayed you? Charles, who's always loved you; Elinor, who was desperate not to hurt you; or Sarah, who lied to you and rejected you?''

"Stop it!" she screamed. "I don't want to hear it." She tried to cover her ears, but with effortless force he pulled her hands away.

"Tough," he said unsympathetically. "I think your real problem is not who betrayed you. I think you're terrified that *you're* going to betray Sarah McDonough. You've kept yourself locked up in your nice, placid world so you won't have to take any chance on being happy, being fulfilled, being a woman. For God's sake, Molly, can't you see that it doesn't have to be like that? She loved you, as best she could, in her own way. You don't have to please her anymore."

Suddenly the last trace of rage vanished, leaving her lost on the edge of the world for a long, breathless moment. And then the tears came—a storm of weeping that washed over her; a cleansing storm of grief and betrayal and letting go. She felt herself enfolded in the warm comfort of James's arms, and she gave herself up to them gladly.

He picked up her trembling, weeping form and carried her through the darkened apartment to her bedroom. Kicking the door shut behind them, he plunged them into inkier darkness, bringing her with him, and still the sobs welled up from a seemingly endless supply.

He made no effort to stop her, reason with her. He seemed content to hold her against him, one hand stroking her tangled hair in rhythmic, soothing strokes. It was what she needed most in the world—

the chance to cry for all the pain and grief she'd kept bottled away.

Finally, after what might have been an eternity, the sobs that racked her body began to fade. Slowly, slowly, they shuddered to a stop. Molly lay there, spent, her head cradled against his now-damp shirt, his arms holding her with gentle strength. As reluctant as she was to leave that comfort, she was afraid to rely on it, and she made a brief attempt to move away.

Immediately his arms tightened around her, keeping her a willing prisoner. "Go to sleep, Molly." His voice was a husky rasp in her ear, tender and concerned. With a sigh of acquiescence she moved closer into the haven of his arms, resting one hand lightly on his shoulder. She was almost asleep when she heard his voice whisper softly through her hair.

"And how did I betray you, Molly?" There was real pain in his voice. Unable to find an answer that wouldn't reveal feelings she couldn't face herself, she snuggled closer, feigning sleep. A few moments later she was no longer pretending.

Her fake sleep hadn't fooled him for a moment. It wasn't until her breathing had slowed to the steady, deep rhythms of real sleep that he moved, flipping the quilt over their entwined bodies. He'd give himself a few hours of holding her vulnerable body in his arms, and no longer. By tomorrow morning her defenses would be firmly in place. Once more he'd have to fight his way through them to reach her.

His next move in their too-elaborate chess game was obvious enough, and yet it was the last thing he wanted to do. Once more he was going to disappear from her life, for a few days or a few weeks if necessary. Just long enough to make her realize that she needed him as much as he needed her.

And if that backfired, he could always try something new, like bribery or forcible abduction, he thought wryly. In the meantime, for the next few hours he'd take what he could get.

Pulling her exhausted body closer into the warm circle of his arms, he willed himself to sleep.

By the time Molly woke up the next morning Elliott was gone. The quilt had been wrapped tightly around her weary body, and the curtains were drawn to keep out the bright morning light. The moment she opened her eyes she knew she was alone in the apartment, and a profound sense of loss overwhelmed her.

Molly emerged from her shower to find the coffee still warm on the stove, but there was no sign of James and no sign of a note. Sighing, Molly poured herself a mug of the strong black brew, padding barefoot into her living room. Still somewhat shell-shocked from the outpouring of long-damned emotions from the night before, she put some soothing Mozart on the stereo, pulled open the drapes to let in the bright autumn sunlight, and curled up on the couch, the mug of coffee warming her hands.

The quilt she was making lay beside her on the sofa, left there when she took off with James for the weekend. The final quilting stitches had been set during the admittedly nervewracking days when she hadn't heard from him, and the binding was half finished. It was perfect, she realized, catching it up with a sigh and pulling out the needle. Almost four years of work were represented in the tiny stitches of the wedding ring pattern, something she'd never repeat. And it wouldn't adorn a wall in her apartment, despite James's sarcastic contention. Nor would it cover their bodies while they made warm, sweet love.

It would be finished in the next few hours, even if her fingers bled, and then sent off by special messenger to the small lodge in Oregon where Charles and Elinor were spending a no-doubt troubled honeymoon. With any luck the peace of mind the wedding quilt would bring would mean even more than the gift itself. She could only hope they knew she was sending her blessing with the quilt.

By six o'clock that evening it had been finished, packed, and sent by the special messenger service the museum usually employed, leaving Molly with nothing to do but sit and wait for James to call. She'd switched from coffee to sherry by midafternoon, vainly trying to concentrate on Thomas Hoving's latest book while she waited. Something must have happened to him, she thought dismally. He couldn't just turn off all that tenderness and compassion so abruptly, despite her lack of appreciation. Could he?

The television relieved some of her uncertainties, even if it gave her tragically unwelcome news. J. E. Seaquist, in ill health during the last few years, had died Sunday morning at age eighty-seven. Details at eleven.

Tears filled her eyes for the sweet old man she'd known for far too brief a time. She grieved for him, and for James, who was clearly much closer to him than a mere employee. And more than anything she wished she could be with him, to comfort him as he had comforted her last night.

But there would undoubtedly be no word from James for several days, she realized with a sudden, desolate sigh, trailing into the kitchen with a listless interest in food. "Damn," she cried weakly into the refrigerator, eyeing the various treats with disfavor. It was already too late. Her body, her mind, her very soul, ached for him. "I don't want to feel like this," she said, slamming the refrigerator door again. "I don't want to need him. Damn, damn, damn!"

Chapter Eighteen

That painful, desolate despair lasted for three days. Her longing for James was compounded by her grief for a gentle old man she had hardly had time to know, and she felt paralyzed by misery and her need for James. Even the joyous, tearful, surprisingly comfortable call from Charles and Elinor only managed a temporary reprieve from her black mood.

By Wednesday evening, when there was still no word from him, her grief and longing began to turn to hurt and anger. By Saturday she was past reasoning with, all her pain and rejection turning into a furious, soul-scorching rage. James's sorrow over J. E.'s death still allowed room for his feelings for her, time for a brief phone call. That is, if he'd ever had any feelings. He'd never put them into words.

"Where are you going now?" Lucia demanded as she slouched up the back steps of the museum on her way back from lunch some ten days after Charles's wedding. "I don't think I've seen you for more than a few moments outside of work for days now. You're gone every lunch time—long lunches, I might add—

and Matheson's getting restless. And you're out every evening as far as I can tell, and when I do see you dragging yourself home, you look as if you can barely walk. You must be having the most torrid affair imaginable, outside of Ian and me, of course. Or else you're getting mugged every night."

"The latter," Molly said sharply, then managed a smile. "Look, if Sebastian calls while I'm out, tell him I've gone to Australia. Betty's been fielding calls for days now, but he's giving her a hard time. You know how persistent he can be. Tell him to go to hell for me, will you?"

"Gladly. But where are you off to this time?" she demanded, curiosity always having been her worst sin. "You can't be seeing James; I know from Ian he's still up north settling the Seaquist estate. James and Ian are coexecutors, you know. So it can't be James that fills your time."

"I'm going to Swensens."

"Pumping iron again?" Lucia cried, a little moue of distaste playing across her elegant face. "I thought you were looking positively emaciated. It's a shame you threw out your designer jeans. I thought you weren't into losing any weight."

Molly shrugged. "I'm not. The weight loss is accidental. And I haven't been pumping iron. Every lunch and evening I've been training with Jee Kow Lung."

"Heavens, what for?" Lucia demanded faintly.

"I'm learning how to beat the hell out of James Elliott," Molly said sweetly and continued on her way.

It was the following Sunday evening, and Molly was busy practicing her moves. The tight black denim jeans she was wearing were a size smaller than usual, her breasts had become fashionably small, and her hollow cheeks matched her haunted eyes. She had been practicing for over an hour now in a vain attempt to work off some of her frustration, when the doorbell rang.

She stalked to the door, hesitating for only a moment. "Who is it?" she called out, willing it to be her nemesis.

Close enough. "Who the hell do you think it is?" Sebastian's voice boomed back. "Haven't I been trying to get in touch with you for the past two weeks? Open up, Molly, there's a love."

With a feral grin Molly slid back the lock. If Sebastian expected to see such dangerous affability in the woman who'd avoided him so assiduously, he merely accepted it as his due, striding into the apartment with his usual bearlike grace.

"Why haven't you returned my phone calls, Molly? You know I can't afford to waste precious time chasing around after you."

"Sorry," she said, unrepentant. Sebastian had already made himself at home, tossing his burly body onto the couch and propping his ragged sneakers on the coffee table. Sighing, she closed the door, locking it again. "And I'd appreciate it if you'd call me M. L. I don't know where everyone's picked up calling me Molly, but I don't like it."

"Got it from James Elliott. Speaking of which, why haven't you returned his phone call either?"

"He wasn't very persistent," Molly shot back, unmoved. "One phone message isn't enough to make me go out of my way, and I haven't heard a word since that message on Thursday. I didn't even recognize the phone number he left."

"Probably it was Cynthia Seaquist's," Sebastian said with damning innocence. "And anyway, your phone's been off the hook since then!"

"Not off the hook," she replied loftily, fighting off the hurt and rage that had suddenly filled her. "Turned off. It's a very convenient option when you don't want to be bothered by eager gentlemen."

Sebastian glared at her from across the room, then his expression softened into one of absent lust. "You look quite pretty, my girl," he said soothingly. "I'm glad to see you've taken my advice and lost some weight. It suits you, darling."

Molly contented herself with a low snarl. "What do you want, Sebastian? I'm not in the mood to entertain."

"You wound me, darling. I just thought—"

"What do you want?" she repeated, an edge to her voice.

With a sigh Sebastian rose, shambling toward her on surprisingly light feet. "I need your help, dear girl. You're the only one I can count on."

"Sebastian, you can't count on me."

"Of course I can. I'm not asking that much of you. Just a word in Elliott's ear, accompanied by your sweet smile."

"My sweet smiles and my words have absolutely no effect on James Elliott," she replied coolly.

"Don't be ridiculous, Molly," Sebastian snapped, no longer so amiable. "Everyone knows the two of you have quite a thing going—you needn't try and hide it from me. I'm above petty jealousy, you know. And it's not as if I'm asking you to prostitute yourself, darling. Just a word or two concerning my over-whelming talent and how deserving I am of my own wing in the Seaquist Museum."

"The Seaquist Museum? What in the world are you talking about?"

"Very convincing," Sebastian sneered. "But you forget I know you. If anyone knows anything about the Seaquist estate, it would be Elliott, and if Elliott knows, you know."

"I realize this may be difficult to understand, Sebastian, but James Elliott is not the confiding type. Besides, I haven't even seen him since the day J. E. died, and I think you'll have to accept the fact that I am even more in the dark about the Seaquist estate than you are."

"Don't lie to me, Molly," he growled, taking a menacing step toward her.

Now was her chance. Molly knew Sebastian inside and out, knew that he wouldn't hurt a fly, much less a healthy female who could scream and fight back. The most he'd ever managed was an overly enthusiastic shove when she'd tried him too far. Nevertheless, Molly squashed her compunctions, caught hold of the hand he'd reached out to her, stepped sideways into him, and neatly flipped all two hundred and forty pounds of him. A moment later he was staring up at her from his supine position on the floor, his eyes glaring at her while he tried to catch his breath.

Molly's exhilaration wiped out any traces of hostility. With a beatific grin she held out a hand to help him to his feet. Shrugging off her assistance with a glare, he brushed himself off, carefully checking for broken bones.

"I'm sorry, Sebastian," she said, her repentance belied by the delight in her expression.

"I'm sorry, Sebastian," he mocked. "The hell you are. Did anyone ever tell you, M. L., that you aren't very feminine? It's damn lucky no bones are broken. If something had happened to my hands, I would have sued you within an inch of your life, and to hell with old friendships. You may not care for your mother's fortune, but it could have comforted me through my declining years of uselessness." He eyed his large hamlike hands warily, as if he expected them to wither in front of him.

Molly could afford to be generous. Surely if she could toss Sebastian's massive bulk so easily, then James's leaner, lighter frame would be a piece of cake. "Your hands are fine, Sebastian. And I'm sorry I can't help you with Elliott, but you'll have to believe me—we haven't spoken in two weeks."

"A lovers' spat?" Sebastian said knowledgeably. "That would explain why he's hanging around Cynthia Seaquist so much nowadays. Not to worry, Molly, these things happen. He'll come around soon enough. And when he does, you might remember—"

"Sebastian, he already recognizes what a great artist you are. I doubt if anything I could say would change his mind one way or the other. And speaking of which, how dare you sell him those two paintings of me? You promised they'd never see the light of day." She advanced on him, her momentary friendliness vanishing.

Sebastian retreated a cautious few paces, raising his hands in supplication. "Watch those hands, Molly," he begged. "You have a right to be angry, I admit it. As a matter of fact, that was the other favor I had to ask of you."

Molly could see the little wheels turning behind Sebastian's limpid eyes. "What are you plotting?" she demanded suspiciously.

"Absolutely nothing!" he swore soulfully. "It's about those nudes I did of you. I would never have sold them to him, except that he told me you two were having an affair. Anyway, I promised I'd have them framed for him. I thought now, while he's still out of town, would be as good a time as any, and I thought you might be able to help me. That way fewer people would actually see them, and I know that's important to you. I've borrowed a van. I just need another pair of hands. Strong hands," he added, flexing his shoulders gingerly.

She only hesitated for a moment. "Certainly," she said with a smile that wouldn't have fooled a ten-year-old. "As long as you're sure he's still gone."

"He'll be at Cynthia's place for a few days longer, I think," Sebastian said innocently. "I wouldn't imagine he'd be in any hurry to get back, if you and he aren't really—"

"We're not," she snapped. "Just let me get my sneakers and a sweater and we can go."

"I'm in no hurry," Sebastian said genially, looking obscurely pleased.

"Well, I am," Molly replied from her bedroom, slipping a very sharp pocket knife into her sweater. "I want to get the job done and get back here before he takes it into his head to finally return home."

"Oh, don't worry about that," Sebastian reassured her from the bedroom door. "He won't show up unexpectedly." And then, oddly enough, he giggled.

Molly turned from her reflection to gaze at him speculatively, then shrugged. Sebastian was a devious soul, but the day he could outwit her would be a cold day in hell. "Let's go."

James's apartment was cool and dark as Molly followed Sebastian's burly figure into its cavernous interior. There was none of the musty, closed-up smell of a place long unoccupied, but Molly attributed that to its wide-open design. She cast only a cursory glance over the apartment as Sebastian flicked the light switch. It was *too* pleasing to her senses—each beautiful piece made her think of the owner with mingled rage and longing.

"How do we find our way upstairs?" Molly questioned with uneasy sharpness. "I want to get this done and be on my way. It's late, I'm tired, and I want to get home to bed." Her nervous, sweat-damp hand toyed with the knife in her sweater pocket.

Sebastian, with maddening deliberation, advanced upon her, a disbelieving expression on his face. "You're kidding me."

"About knowing my way to James Elliott's bedroom? Afraid not." She tossed her mane of hair airily. "Reports of our so-called affair have been greatly exaggerated."

"You mean you never slept with him?" he demanded, looking put out.

Molly didn't waste her time trying to decipher his strange reactions. "That's none of your business," she snapped.

Sebastian breathed a sigh of relief. "I knew I couldn't be wrong. It's hard to mistake when someone is mooning around like a lovesick sheep."

"Damn it, you think you know me so well! You might find you're mistaken about me and my emotions. You never used to be very astute at reading me." Avoiding his gaze, she picked up a figurine, a charming piece of early French ceramic ware, her knowledgeable eyes running over the pure, graceful lines of it.

"I wasn't talking about you, dear girl," Sebastian said lightly. "I haven't seen you in weeks. I was referring to James Elliott's irritable abstraction."

She looked up then. "Maybe you bring it out in him," she suggested with the ghost of a smile.

"Maybe," Sebastian said doubtfully. "However, I don't think—"

To Molly's complete, benumbed horror, Sebastian's rambling conversation was interrupted by the unmistakable sound of a key in the lock. She stood there in the shadows, rooted to the spot, the ceramic in her hand, as the door opened and James Elliott and Cynthia Seaquist walked in, laughing, with the low, comfortable laugh of long familiarity.

The sound was like a blow to Molly's stomach, coupled with the sight of him. He was always handsomer than she remembered, she thought miserably. That aloof, slightly arrogant face was smiling down at Cynthia Seaquist the way it used to smile down at her, and his lean strong body in the elegant dark suit sent waves of longing through her.

James looked up from his companion and saw Sebastian's still figure. "You again, Sebastian? What are you doing here?" he demanded wearily, in the tone of one used to such impositions. "Kicked out by your most recent lady friend? You can borrow the couch again, but I warn you, I've got a lot to do—"

Cynthia, to Molly's intense regret, met her with a friendly smile across the darkened room. "I think you misunderstood the situation, Jamie. He's brought his lady friend with him." She was watching Molly out of sweet, quizzical blue eyes, and Molly realized miserably that it would be impossible to hate such a warm, friendly creature, even one as pretty as Cynthia Seaquist.

James had suddenly become very still, rather like a fox whose lair had been invaded, she thought fancifully. His eyes were dark and glittering in the shadows as they met Molly's. She could read no expression in them whatsoever. "That's not Sebastian's lady friend, Cynthia. Or, at least, not anymore. That's Molly McDonough. Better known as Dr. M. L. McDonough of the Museum of American Arts. Molly, this is Cynthia Seaquist." He performed the introductions in a toneless voice, his eyes wary.

"I'm so glad to meet you," Cynthia said with real

warmth that added to Molly's confusion. "I've heard so much about you, both from Jamie and from people in the art world. My uncle was very impressed with you, you know. That was all he could talk about the day he died. He took great pleasure in meeting and talking with you."

Jamie? Molly thought with amazement. "You're very kind," she murmured inanely, wishing she were anywhere in the world but standing in that apartment, exchanging polite chitchat.

"Are you planning to throw that figurine at me, Molly?" James drawled, putting a proprietary arm around Cynthia's slender form and pulling her close to his frame. "It's a very rare piece and quite valuable."

"I know that as well as you do." Gingerly she replaced it. "It belongs in a museum."

"You *would* say that." He bent his most seductive look down at the petite woman by his side. "Molly thinks it sinful for private collectors to own anything worthwhile. She thinks it should be moldering away in museums, and that it should all belong to the people. I wonder if the people are properly grateful for her concern?"

Cynthia was looking up at James with undisguised amazement. "Are you out of your mind, Jamie?" she demanded hotly, pulling herself out of his possessive embrace. "You should know by now that I don't like being used." She stalked to the door, pausing long enough to smile apologetically at Molly's motionless figure.

"I'm sorry about this, Dr. McDonough. I don't know what's got into this wretched man, but it was a pleasure to meet you after I've heard so much about you." Before Molly could reply, she was gone, the door shut behind her.

For the first time a surprisingly silent Sebastian spoke. "Molly and I just came to pick up the nudes, old man. You remember I promised I'd get them properly framed for you."

"I don't remember any such thing," James snapped, his eyes never leaving Molly's still figure. "I like them the way they are."

"Well, then, perhaps Molly and I should leave," he said with a sly smile, heading toward the door and gesturing for Molly to follow.

"Wait a minute," James said hastily. "Maybe you're right. After all, you painted them."

"I knew you'd see it my way," Sebastian said in dulcet tones, and Molly had the uneasy conviction that something more was going on between the two men than she realized. However, she wasn't about to object when her mission was so near completion.

James played right into her hands. "Why don't you go up and see what you think, Molly?" he suggested, suddenly affable. "After all, as the model, you ought to have some say in the matter, and you have an excellent eye. Sebastian and I have a few things to work out and then we'll be up."

The look she cast him was full of chilly disdain. "I'm afraid I don't know how to get to your bedroom."

"She really doesn't?" Sebastian marveled boisterously. "Who would have thought it? You must be slipping, old boy."

James studiously ignored him. "The stairway is beyond the left-hand door in the hallway. I'll be right up."

Molly took her dismissal with a dangerous smile, finding the staircase with no difficulty. She had the penknife out and ready. She was damned if he was going to sit in his bedroom and gloat over his triumph. Those pictures were never meant to be seen by anyone, and she was going to make sure of it. If there was a chance to deck James Elliott in the bargain, so much the better.

Determinedly she ignored the bedroom, the wide bed covered with a quilt so old and so beautiful that Molly felt a pang of covetousness. She had always had a weakness for quilts. The rugs beneath her feet were very old Oriental prayer rugs, and the highly polished pale oak floorboards gleamed beneath her sneakered feet. There was a warm, safe feel to the bedroom, as if it were tucked away from the world and all its problems. The effect was increased by the chocolate-brown walls and small, diamond-paned casement windows that let in the fitful city lights. The two oversize flamboyant nudes were the only touch of modern elegance.

It had been a long time since she'd seen them, and she paused in front of them, fingering the open knife. They were very good, she realized for the first time, and embarrassingly erotic. She eyed them from an objective distance, imagining it was some other lush creature staring out so defiantly at the world. She was glad of that defiance. Every time James Elliott looked at that painted face, she had been telling him to go to hell. It was almost worth leaving them intact.

But that was *her* lushly nude body beneath that defiant face, and there was no way James Elliott would ever possess it again, on or off canvas. With slow, deliberate steps she forced herself toward the paintings, knife upraised.

Chapter Nineteen

"Don't you dare." James's voice came from directly behind her.

She hesitated for only a moment. Leaping forward, she went straight for one of the portraits. James was there ahead of her, her knife-wielding hand caught in a bone-crushing grip as he whirled her around to face him. The knife clattered to the floor, dropped by nerveless fingers, as she glared up into his glittering, fury-filled eyes.

Now was her chance, she recognized triumphantly, giving up the destruction of her paintings without another thought. Now was the time for revenge.

With lethal, practiced grace she stepped sideways into his body, every nerve and muscle prepared. A moment later she found herself flat on her back on the soft bed, with James's larger, stronger body covering hers, pressing her down against the antique quilt.

"Where did you learn that little trick?" he demanded huskily, his face so close to hers that his breath was warm on her skin. Hastily she averted her head, trying to fight the treacherous surge of longing that filled her at the weight of his body on hers, the clean masculine smell of him, the warmth of his breath. His heart was beating in slow, steady beats against her breasts, and her heart joined in a counterpoint that meshed with his.

"It didn't work, did it?" she countered stonily, determined to remain unmoved.

"No, it didn't. Sorry to disappoint you, but my shadowy past includes a passing knowledge of martial arts." He moved slightly, trying to make himself more comfortable, and his hands brushed the taut peaks of her breasts. "If you'd tried it with almost anyone else, you would probably have had no trouble throwing them."

"Don't be so condescending," she muttered. "I threw Sebastian."

He laughed, his body pressing more intimately against hers, and she realized with a sudden surge of hot longing that he was aroused; the feel of his body against hers left no doubt whatsoever. "That must have been quite a sight," he murmured, his mouth moving to her exposed neck and planting a light, experimental kiss there. "Was his dignity shattered?"

"No, but he was sure his hands were permanently crippled," she returned in a strangled voice. His mouth had continued a gentle, exploratory trail down the side of her neck to her open blouse. His stronger body held her immobile; there was nothing she could do but lie there and try not to react to the teasing pressure of his mouth. "Where is Sebastian, anyway?"

"I sent him home. He'd already done what he set out to do. Did you realize your ex-lover is a determined matchmaker?"

"Only when he thinks it's going to benefit him. He thinks I can influence you into further subsidizing his career. I tried to explain to him that I have no influence over you whatsoever." Her voice was only slightly breathless.

He made no response to that deliberately provocative statement. "Why didn't you return my phone call?" he whispered at the cleft of her breasts.

"Damn you, why should I?" she cried helplessly, trying to squirm out of his embrace. He held her completely immobile as one hand reached between them and cupped her soft breast. "It took you ten days to bother to get in touch with me, ten days of waiting, of—" She broke off, determined not to expose the extent of her vulnerability. "Why shouldn't you wait, as I had to?" she finished, her husky voice deceptively calm.

Slowly he raised his head, looking down at her troubled face, and a wry, self-deprecating smile flitted over his mouth. "Just because I'm a turkey doesn't mean you have to follow suit." Somehow his hands had moved up to cradle her head, the thumbs lightly stroking the sides of her face. "I could come up with a dozen plausible excuses for not calling you, for not coming to see you."

"I'm not asking for excuses," she said stubbornly, fighting the insidious effect the slow, sensuous stroking was having on her body. "I have no claim on you."

"But that's where you're wrong," he said, brushing his lips softly against hers. "Since I met you I haven't a soul to call my own. And quite frankly, dear lady, it scares the hell out of me." He moved his mouth lower, dancing over her stubborn chin. "I had planned to seduce you, not fall in love with you." He felt her sudden start beneath him and he dropped his mouth lightly, reassuringly, on hers.

"James," she gasped in a sudden rush of fear and hope. The barriers of her distrust were slowly crumbling as she lay there, imprisoned by the lean, warm strength of him. She wanted them to crumble, willed the last shreds of doubt to dissolve, but they clung stubbornly. "James—" she began, but his mouth silenced hers.

In silence she twisted her arms out from their prison beneath his strong body. In silence she slid them up his body and around his neck as she opened her mouth willingly beneath his. If she couldn't answer him with words, she could at least respond with her body, and her tongue met his in a silent language that promised and received love.

Rolling to one side, he drew her willing body with him, his hand urgent with her clothes as his mouth teased and cajoled her flesh. With deft dispatch he unbuttoned the clinging silk blouse, unfastened the front clasp of her bra, and pushed the clothes off her shoulders. "You've gotten too skinny," he murmured against her skin. "What have you been doing to yourself since I saw you?" His hand was already trailing across her flat stomach and working on the snap of her jeans.

"Sulking," she said with a weak laugh as he pulled the jeans off her hips. "And practicing judo."

His jacket sailed onto the floor, followed by his tie and shirt. The sound of his belt buckle being unfastened sent such a wave of longing through her that she closed her eyes. "I promise to let you throw me next time," he whispered. "As long as *you* land on top of me."

She opened her eyes then, to see him kneeling over her, gloriously, uncompromisingly nude. "It's a deal," she said slowly, holding out her arms to him.

If the feel of their clothed bodies in close embrace had been demoralizing, the sudden descent of his warm smooth muscled frame destroyed her last tiny shred of self-control. She was afire with longing, aching for the touch that had seemed forever denied her.

But James was not about to be rushed. Catching her slender wrists in one large, strong hand, he pulled her arms over her head, leaving her lying there, exposed and vulnerable to his stormy eyes and hungry mouth. He watched her for a long, breathless moment as she writhed slightly, and the feel of his hot gaze on her was an aphrodisiac. When his head finally lowered, she met his mouth with desperate excitement, her tongue joining with his, her whole soul and body seeming to concentrate in her mouth.

Too soon he pulled his lips away, and her groan of passion and loss seemed to inflame him further. But he was determined to slow the pace. With maddening deliberation his mouth trailed hot, damp kisses on her cheekbones, her eyelids, her jaw, and then began a slow descent down the sensitive column of her throat, across her collarbone, to capture the rosy peak of one already aroused breast. She arched into his mouth, her hands still held captive in his iron grip, a small whimper escaping her lips as his tongue slowly flicked the turgid nipple. There seemed to be a straight line of fire from that nipple to the heat in her loins, and she jerked with the exquisite torment of it. And then he moved to her other breast, performing the same wicked magic, until Molly was afraid she might weep with longing.

"James, please," she begged, writhing beneath his touch, longing for release, desperate to have him move up and cover her with his strong body.

"Not this time, Molly," he murmured, his breath warm and tickling against her stomach. "Tonight we're going to take our time." Suddenly her wrists were released, and she reached down to pull him up and over her. But James had other ideas. Cupping her buttocks in both strong hands, he moved his mouth down to capture the very heart of her femininity.

At the first touch of his mouth a low wail escaped Molly's lips, and her fingers dug helplessly into James's strong shoulders. The feel of his rough tongue thrusting into her further melted the last bit of her inhibitions, and when the sudden, unexpected, mind-shattering release came, her nails dug in far enough to draw blood, and in the distance she heard her voice sob out his name.

It seemed years before reality returned. She was lying cradled against his aroused body, and those clever hands were stroking her still-trembling body with sure strokes. As strength returned to her limbs, determination returned with it, and slowly she rose out of the circle of his arms. His eyes were hooded with passion, a curious, tentative half smile playing about his mouth.

"My turn," she said softly, pushing him over on his back with gentle force. Holding his hands down by his sides, she began to kiss him, her eager mouth traveling over the ridges and planes of his face, nibbling at the lower edge of his lips, trailing her tongue teasingly against his strong white teeth. Before he could respond, she moved away, determined to taste all of him. His skin was warm, damp, and slightly salty from his recent exertions, and the faint traces of his well-remembered after-shave brought a host of erotic memories.

She loved the smoothness of his skin, the darkly tanned, leanly muscled flesh that pulsed beneath her exploring mouth. Slowly she trailed her tongue across one flat male nipple, and was delighted to see it respond much as hers had to his more experienced mouth. And then she moved to his other nipple, her hands leaving their ineffectual hold on his wrists, and his large, strong hands reached up and covered her shoulders.

"What are you trying to do to me?" he gasped as her mouth trailed lower to the tiny tracing of hair across his flat stomach. Her tongue dipped lightly into his navel, and his entire body twitched convulsively.

"I'm just trying to show you how much I appreciate your finer points," she said lightly. This was the difficult part. Moving back slightly, she let her hands move slowly, deliberately, downward to capture the raging heat of his desire.

"Molly..." His voice was both desperate and pleading, and she hesitated no longer. Leaning forward, she placed her lips on him, her mouth moist and welcoming and sweetly experimental.

After a long, delicious, yet too-short moment, she felt his hands tighten on her shoulders, and slowly, carefully, he pulled her away, suddenly taking the control he had willingly abdicated. He rolled her onto her back, his body following, as deft hands parted her legs.

She raised her hips gladly to meet his first thrust, glorying in the feel of his strength as it filled her. Her legs were wrapped around his lean, plunging body as she met him, thrust for thrust, the rhythm washing over her in waves of transcending desire. His hands caught her hips, his fingers digging into the soft flesh, as he drove in deeply. And then he was lost, his voice calling her name in the darkness. And she followed him over the waterfall of desire into the rapids below, where she was content to float, sated, in his arms.

He fell asleep on top of her. She couldn't really blame him—he had looked exhausted when he first walked in this evening. Slowly, carefully, she moved from underneath him. He only woke for a moment to look at her out of surprisingly sharp eyes before falling back with a deep sigh.

Molly sat beside him on the bed, staring down at his sleeping form. And then she looked around the dimly lit bedroom, the pile of clothes on the floor, the two sleek nudes on the wall, the perfection of his bachelor taste. Carefully she stifled the sudden upsurge of doubt as she crept off the bed and sorted her discarded clothes from his.

"Don't be ridiculous," she admonished herself as she trailed downstairs with her clothes held in front of her nude body. "He said he loved you. He wouldn't have said it if he didn't mean it. He's not a person to lie." It was perhaps unfortunate that at that moment her gaze would fall on the pierced-tin pie safe, but determinedly she banished her doubts as effectively as she washed the traces of their lovemaking from her body. Bruises were already beginning to form on her white hips, and she viewed the dark spots with a tender smile. He'd bear her mark too—she'd tasted his blood from the scratches on his shoulders. Let him try to explain *that* to someone.

Now, why should she think that? Who would he be explaining it to? He loved her.

Molly was taking the first, tentative sips of the scalding black coffee she had made when she wandered into the living area and over to the large nineteenth-century library table that was far neater than her own work space. Never one to control her curiosity, she peered at the neatly piled papers. J. E. Seaquist's papers, she realized, with his will on top. It was easy enough to recognize the blue-backed form of a legal document. Decisively she turned her back on temptation, strolling over to the floor-to-ceiling windows.

It was more than noble, she thought with a sigh. Ever since J. E.'s death, speculation and rumor had been rife in the Bay Area art world. The disposal of a collection the size of J. E. Seaquist's would have international repercussions, and Molly was just as curious as anyone else. Especially considering that several pieces in that collection should have been hers.

Well, so what if it was a rotten, devious, and unethical thing to do? she thought as she moved back to the desk. James Elliott was just as capable of that sort of thing. A tiny peek at the will would satisfy her curiosity and no one would be any the wiser. Would it really go to Seaquist's nine nieces and nephews, to be scattered and dispersed among the greedy hands of private collectors? Or had Seaquist some other plan in mind? J. E. had appeared to be a man of both sense and mischief—surely he'd be more imaginative. Banishing her last trace of conscience, she picked up the blue-lined will.

Slowly her fingers turned to ice as her mind tried to assimilate the words. Finally, the truth sank in, and with it self-disgust. How could she have been so weak as to let him get close again? Stupid, stupid, stupid!

"Find out anything interesting?" James's voice came from across the room, and slowly Molly lowered the sheets of paper. Her other hand was still clenched around the coffee mug, so tightly, she had the absent fear that the pottery might be crushed in her hand.

"I hadn't got to the good parts yet," Molly said in a controlled voice. "Just the whereases and therefores, none of the bequests."

James was fool enough to relax. "Then you haven't learned anything you don't already know," he said easily, moving across the room and plucking the will from her nerveless fingers. "Don't be too inquisitive,

Molly Bloom; you'll find out all the details soon enough."

He was very handsome, standing there with his navy velour robe draped around his spare tall body. Molly recognized his attraction with an added fillip of fury.

"Oh, that's where you're wrong," she said smoothly. "You somehow neglected to mention that J. E. Seaquist was James Elliott Seaquist. Your uncle, I believe? And I would presume you're his heir, not his glorified gopher?"

He had enough sense to eye her warily. "There are nine heirs," he said finally. "And I'm only one of them. That is, if J. E.'s preferred plans don't go through. Look, I'm sorry I didn't tell you, but after all, what does it really matter? I just got so used to keeping it a secret, I didn't think to mention it to you."

"Didn't think to mention it," she mimicked, and then flung the contents of her coffee mug at him.

Although no longer scalding, it was hot enough to be uncomfortable as it drenched his chest, and his language was worse than Molly's most colorful efforts. Darting past him, she grabbed her sweater from the couch, her face set in rigid, angry lines.

"Don't you think you're overreacting?" he managed, wiping his face with the kimono-style sleeve.

"No." She yanked on the sweater with rough hands and belted it around her waist. "You lied to me. I can't bear being lied to."

"What if I promised never to do it again?" he attempted with a winning smile.

"Go to hell."

"But I love you."

That was the final straw. "I don't believe you," she snapped.

"Why? Are you afraid to?" he taunted. "Isn't this a convenient excuse to run again? It's a lot easier to convince yourself that I'm lying, that I used you."

She stared at him for a long silent moment. Then, with mesmerizing deliberation, she reached down and picked up the rare antique figurine she'd admired earlier and smashed it against the wall. Without another word she stormed out, slamming the door behind her.

James looked from the door to the smashed pieces of the priceless figurine, and a smile lit his dark face. "Bless your heart, Molly," he murmured, his voice thick with relief. "You *do* love me."

Chapter Twenty

"Congratulations, McDonough," Dr. Matheson barked at her as he strode down the hall. He was in one of his youthful-vigor kicks, which involved racing pell-mell down the hallways, whistling Beethoven quite loudly, and never carrying on a conversation while standing still. His more elderly colleagues considered this the most trying of his many personae, but Molly, immersed as she had been for the last few weeks in her own uncertain emotions, found it singularly inoffensive. "Quite a feather in your cap, and in the museum's too, of course. Well done."

"Uh...thank you." She wasn't quite sure what feat she had supposedly accomplished. The acquisition of a rather nice Paul Revere teapot was a good move, but nothing spectacular. No nefarious robber baron had appeared from out of nowhere to outbid her, and nothing had clouded the piece's authenticity. It was all quite boringly predictable, as everything had been in the past weeks since she had seen James Elliott. Of course, there was no connection between the two, she maintained staunchly, even to herself.

Dr. Matheson was already halfway down the hall. "Keep up the good work, McDonough. Hurry back. We'll miss you." On that cryptic utterance he disappeared through the swinging doors at the end of the hallway, whistling noisily.

"Curiouser and curiouser," Molly mused as she continued down the hallway to her office. The sight that met her there was enough to make her stop dead in her tracks, sorely tempted to turn on her heel and head back in the opposite direction and out of the museum. But she wasn't about to give James Elliott that satisfaction. Particularly not with an audience comprised of Ian Henderson and Lucia Caldwell.

Throwing back her shoulders, she strode into her office, armed with a chilly smile. "To what do I owe this unexpected honor?"

"*Intrusion* is a more likely term," James drawled from his perch by the window.

"I thought I should be polite," Molly replied, keeping her voice coolly courteous. "How are you, Ian? Did you enjoy yourself at the Caldwells' house last weekend? Lucia's parents are delightful, I think."

Ian cleared his throat. There was a professional cast to his boyishly attractive face, one that Molly hadn't seen before, and for the first time she realized he could look like a lawyer. "We had a great time," he said just the tiny bit ponderously, the weight of his profession sitting heavily on his shoulders. "But we've come on a professional matter. Perhaps we'd best get that out of the way before we socialize."

"I have no desire to socialize with the present company." She had to pass damnably close to James's ar-

rogantly lounging figure, and her very skin seemed to
burn with the heat of his nearness. She managed it
with deceptive grace, moving to her seat behind the
cluttered desk and sinking down, her tightly clenched
fists hidden in her lap. She had been prepared to slug
him if he'd even touched her. The heat from his
mocking, caressing gray eyes was physical torment
enough.

"So what is this professional matter that's so important?" she questioned, tipping back in her chair and
wishing she smoked. A chocolate or two would have
done wonders for her equilibrium, but she had lost
interest in food recently. "And why are you here, Lucia?"

"I'm moral support," she replied with an uneasy
grin.

"For whom? Them or me?"

Lucia shrugged. "I'd back you in a fight anytime."

"Is this a fight, Ian?" She still studiously ignored
the silent figure by the window.

Once more Ian cleared his throat, obviously ill at
ease. "As you no doubt already know, I represent
both the late James Elliott Seaquist and James Elliott
the Fourth. It's a matter of great concern—"

"The fourth?" Molly echoed, managing a beautifully mocking glance at James's impassive face.
"My, my, how elegant. Are you suing me for smash-
ing that figurine, James the Fourth? I'd be glad to
pay whatever price you put on it. It was more than
worth it."

A brief, enigmatic smile lit his face. "The figurine
is the least of my worries, Molly Bloom. Why don't

you be quiet for once, just long enough to hear what Ian has to say?"

Carefully Molly bit back the retort that rose to her lips. There was nothing James would like more than to goad her, and she was not about to let him know how much power he had over her. "All right," she said with a questionable amiability. "What have you come to see me about, Ian?"

"It concerns the estate of James Elliott Seaquist," he began portentously, and Molly settled back for the duration, keeping her face averted from James's observant gray eyes. "I won't bother you with all the legal technicalities, as you'll probably want to see a copy of the will yourself. The main thrust of it is this: The bulk of the Seaquist estate, including his extensive art collection, has been left in trust to form the Seaquist Museum Foundation. It was Seaquist's plan to set up living museums—perfectly restored houses and estates where people could come and live among the antiques and works of art. For example, his first furnished house is an eighteenth-century Spanish hacienda in Juanito, California. It's been lovingly restored with complete historical accuracy—no electricity or plumbing, of course, and all the paintings the original owners brought with them from Spain. The closets will be filled with clothes from the period—usually reproductions, I'm afraid, since twentieth-century Americans tend to be a great deal larger than eighteenth-century Spaniards. There's also a miner's cabin near the original Sutter's Mill, a gingerbread gothic in Colorado, a small castle moved stone by stone from England and being reassembled in Idaho, and more are planned. If everything goes through, of course.''

"Who'll stay in these places? Scholars, researchers, students?'' Molly questioned, fascinated despite herself.

"And families, honeymoon couples, retirees. They'll be open to anyone with a genuine love and appreciation for history. On a sliding scale, of course. Mr. Seaquist is leaving the whole operation extremely well endowed.'' Ian cleared his throat again. "Well, Molly, what do you think?''

She hesitated, turning the idea over in her mind, determined to find some major objection or drawback. She turned an accusing eye to James's impassive figure. "Is that what you've been amassing artwork for?''

"Guilty as charged. Sebastian is quite desperate to have his own wing at the main branch. Sea Tor will be turned into an art museum specializing in American painting and sculpture, and Coddaire's been lobbying for the center banquet hall.''

"Sebastian having known about this plan for weeks, I presume?'' she questioned coldly. "That's to be expected. Why are you telling me all this now?'' She turned back to Ian. "How do I fit in with all this?''

"That's entirely up to you. You still haven't told us what you think of the idea of living museums.''

"Whose idea was it originally?'' she hedged. "Or need I bother to ask?''

"You've got it, Molly,'' James verified lightly. "It was my idea in the first place, based on a hatred of traditional museums and the reluctant conviction that art really should belong to the people, and not from a safe, sterilized distance."

She looked at Ian, deliberately turning her slender back on an amused James. "I think it's a very good idea," she said honestly enough, shocking herself and everyone in the room. "So what's it got to do with me?"

Ian cast an imploring glance at James, but got no help from that quarter. "There's a catch in the provisions of the will. James Elliott was the only one in his family that J. E. had any faith in. The museum trust only holds if James heads the foundation, with a specified second in command and a staff of his choice."

Molly was way ahead of him. "No way."

"Now, hear me out, Molly," Ian said desperately. "There's a great deal involved here, more than you imagine. You can't just dismiss it out of hand. You haven't even heard our offer—"

"I've heard enough. No."

"Just hold on a minute, M. L.," Lucia broke in. "You haven't given Ian a chance to explain. They don't want you to quit your job—just a leave of absence to help set up the museums. Matheson thinks it's a splendid opportunity—both for you and the Museum of American Arts's prestige."

"And who would take over my job while I did all this?" she snapped.

"I would," Lucia replied, eyes modestly downcast. "Please, M. L., consider it. Think of the opportunities it would offer. Seaquist has been collecting for over sixty years now, and only a small portion has been cataloged. It would be like a giant treasure hunt. Any other curator would give their souls for a chance like this."

"Then you do it."

"It wasn't offered to her," James said flatly. "She hasn't got your expertise."

Molly whirled around to meet his unreadable gaze. "Aren't you going to add your blandishments to all this?" she demanded caustically.

"Certainly not. The decision is yours." His voice was almost bored.

"And if I say no to this fabulous offer?"

"Simple enough." James moved away from the window and came to her desk, leaning across the clutter. "If I don't get the staff I want, I won't head the museum. If I don't head the museum, the trust is broken, and the estate reverts to his nine nieces and nephews. Myself among them."

"Wouldn't you prefer that?" She couldn't control her curiosity any longer. "Wouldn't one ninth of the Seaquist estate and art treasures be far more valuable than whatever salary you'd get as head of the Seaquist museums?"

"Considering that I would get no salary whatsoever, I would say so," he said wryly. "But the fact of the matter is, I have no need for any more money. I have quite sufficient for my needs."

"Oh, yes, the power of inherited wealth and trust funds," she said snottily, blithely ignoring her own inheritance, which lay essentially untouched in the bank. She watched his eyes narrow in sudden temper.

"My uncle trusted me because I was the only one

of his heirs who knew how to make their own way," he snapped. "And I can still do it, without his inheritance or the museums either."

Looking at his austere, determined face, she didn't for one moment doubt him. "You want me to believe that if I refuse to take a leave of absence to become your assistant you'll invalidate the will?"

"Yes."

She believed him. She already knew that James Elliott could be a frighteningly determined man. He would be more than capable of throwing the whole thing away rather than let her defeat him.

"You don't really leave me a choice, do you?" she acquiesced with little grace.

"No, I don't." Luckily for the state of his shins, James didn't gloat over his triumph. "Ian will draw up a contract, and it will be waiting on your desk at my office tomorrow for you to sign."

"Tomorrow? Surely you don't expect me to just drop everything here and start—"

"Lucia can handle it," James said flatly. "You're overqualified for your job as it is. Look at it this way: The sooner you start, the sooner you can finish and be rid of my onerous company."

"Which I'm sure will please you just as much," she shot back. "What I don't understand is why you're insisting on me, when you obviously have as little desire to spend time with me as I have with you."

For a brief moment a fire burned in those silver-gray eyes, a white-hot flame of desire that sent an answering shaft of heat through her loins. And then, just as suddenly, those fires were banked, hidden behind hooded eyes. "Because you're the best qualified for the job. J. E. agreed with my assessment," he informed her coldly, as if that shared passion was no more than a figment of her imagination. "I suppose there's someone else, either here or on the east coast, who'd be just as capable, but I can't afford to waste my time looking for them. You'll suit me just fine." As far as she could tell, there was no double entendre in that last phrase.

For the fourth or fifth time Ian cleared his throat, and Molly stifled the urge to snap at him. "Well, why don't the four of us go out to lunch to celebrate the agreement? I know of a marvelous sushi bar just a few blocks away."

Molly had opened her mouth to flatly refuse when James broke in, greatly to her annoyance. "I'm sorry, Ian. I have other plans." There was no regret in that even voice. "I'll be expecting you tomorrow, Molly."

She was tempted to click her heels and say yes, sir, with an appropriate salute. She contented herself with a cool, dignified nod, but he was already gone.

"Damn that man!" she cried in heartfelt anger.

"When are you two going to get off your high horse?" Lucia demanded. "Or is it high horses? Whatever."

"I don't know what you mean." Molly's husky voice was stubborn.

"Listen, kiddo, I know more about steamy passion than just about anyone, but it would take a fool not to notice the heat generated between the two of you. Why, that look you two gave each other awhile back almost made me blush. Why don't you give up and admit you want him? He's obviously crazy about you."

"Obviously. He could hardly bear to tear himself away just now," she said caustically.

"You weren't terribly encouraging. If he hadn't spoken first, I'm sure you would have refused to come. I could see your face screwing up to say no, and I'm sure James could too. It's no wonder he spiked your guns by refusing first."

"And I'm sure you're reading too much into the whole situation," Molly shot back, quelling the tiny surge of stubborn hope.

"And I'm sure I'm starving," Ian wailed, his lawyer's mien dropped with the cessation of business. "Could we continue with the loves of James and Molly over sushi before I expire?"

"Romantic, isn't he?" Lucia said fondly, her dry tone belied by the softness in her eyes. "Come on, M. L., let's go. You need some advice to the lovelorn from Dear Lucia."

"I need no such thing. I need to brief you on the thousand and one things hanging fire at the museum," she said, grabbing her leather shoulder bag from the bottom drawer. "And Ian doesn't want to hear about the trials and tribulations of M. L. McDonough."

"I'm not really interested in the trials and tribulations of the Museum of American Arts either," he admitted plaintively. "However, I should have no difficulty immersing myself in sushi."

"Bless you, darling, what a lovely thought." Lucia bestowed an appreciative kiss on his brow. "You see why I hung on to this one, kiddo. Now we just have to get you settled as nicely, and we can all live happily ever after."

"Why, Lucia, my love, is that a proposal?" Ian's voice trailed behind them as he struggled to keep up with the two women.

"Once I get Molly here taken care of, it is," she said blithely.

"In that case, you can count on my assistance," he swore, slipping his arms through theirs. "You'll find I can be very informative about James and his scarlet past."

"And I've already planned his scarlet future. Don't worry, darling, we'll take care of everything," Lucia told Molly.

"That's what I'm afraid of," Molly said soberly.

Chapter Twenty-One

Molly looked forward to the next few weeks with a strange mixture of resentment, anticipation, trepidation, and an overwhelming thirst for revenge. That her tenure with the newly formed Seaquist Museum Foundation would be a short one, she had little doubt. She could be far more trouble than she was worth, and from now on there would be no holding back with James Elliott. She would devote all her energies to making him heartily sorry he ever cast those cold gray eyes in her direction. She could be a formidable opponent when she wished, and even if James had up till now found effective ways to get the better of her, the truce was over. It was a war, and she looked forward to the next battle with real enthusiasm.

Unfortunately, James Elliott had used the one tactic against which she had no defense. When she arrived at the small elegant corporate offices the next morning, armed for battle in her prettiest raw silk suit, she found her nemesis had disappeared without a trace.

The shark-faced office manager had eyed her with obvious disapproval, settling her into her new office with a reluctant efficiency. "No, Dr. McDonough, I have absolutely no idea when Mr. Elliott is expected back," she said in a polite, colorless voice. "He could be gone a week or a month—there's no telling."

"Isn't that rather inefficient?" Molly met her lack of warmth with an equal coolness. "What if someone needs to get in touch with him concerning the Seaquist collection or his uncle's estate?"

"Those who need to get in touch with him personally will know how to do so," she said shortly. "The others will simply have to make do with you." Her expression left little doubt as to how much use that would be.

"And I'm not considered of sufficient importance to be privy to his whereabouts?"

"Apparently not." Miss Bateson allowed herself a small, sour smile. She was probably near forty years old, though she looked ten years older, and her strictly tailored clothes on her ruthlessly slender body would have done credit to a corpse. "The folders on your left are the records concerning the hacienda in Juanito and the Steele house in Oregon. He suggested you might familiarize yourself with these projects to begin with, the first being near completion and the latter in its earliest stages."

Molly looked around the wide expanse of her elegant modern office, at the broad, clear top of her desk, and sighed. For the time being she was trapped, and there was nothing she could do but try to pass the time until Elliott chose to reappear and she could end this charade. Picking up a thick folder, she tried one last time for an ingratiating smile at the cold stick of a woman opposite her.

"Thank you for your assistance, Ms Bateson. I'm sure there's plenty here to keep me busy for a while, at least. I just hope Mr. Elliott hasn't chosen this occasion for one of his lengthier disappearances."

"I'm sure I couldn't say, Dr. McDonough," the woman replied repressively. "And my name is *Miss* Bateson."

Molly smiled at the woman with great sweetness. "You make your political statements, and I'll make mine, *Ms* Bateson."

The only answer was the decisive closing of the door behind that ramrod-straight back. The door was too heavy and too well hung to offer the satisfaction of a slam, and Molly then and there decided never to live in a house where the doors wouldn't provide a soul-satisfying slam when needed. Sighing, she turned to the information at hand.

It was some nine days later when word from James Elliott finally filtered down to her. In the meantime she had learned everything she could about the various estates in Seaquist's living museum complex, the hacienda in Juanito proving an especial favorite of hers. She had approved the bids for the renovation of the Denver mansion, and she had begun cataloging the almost overwhelming collection of jumbled artwork in the long-closed Seaquist mansion on Telegraph Hill. And she found, when she wasn't thinking of James's elegant body with mingled longing and fury, that she was enjoying herself more than she ever had in a job, and the thought added to her disgruntled state of mind.

It was early Friday afternoon when Norma Bateson made her appearance in Molly's office. The entire contents of the three hacienda files were spread out over her desk, and Molly looked up as a small moan of despair came from the ruthlessly neat woman's compressed lips.

"May I help you, Ms Bateson?" she inquired coolly. Hostilities had continued unabated between the two women, despite Molly's periodic attempts at conciliation.

Obviously unable to control herself, the woman jerked out, "I hope you know which files those papers belong to, Doctor."

Molly's smile was sunshine itself. "Well, I'm sure if I can't remember, you'll be able to reconstruct them."

"Were you looking for something in particular?"

"As a matter of fact, I was. Have you seen the master list of the paintings? I can't seem to find it, and it's an important addendum to the brochure."

"The brochure is due at the printers first thing Monday morning," Norma Bateson pointed out with certain grim satisfaction. "Mr. Elliott won't like it if there's a delay."

About to inform Ms Bateson what Mr. Elliott could do with the brochure, Molly took a deep, calming breath. "I'm well aware of that," she replied with only a trace of the irritation she was feeling. "And the brochure will be there. What did you want?"

"Mr. Elliott called this morning and left a message for you. I thought it would be better if I delivered it personally rather than entrusting one of the secretaries."

"He called?" Molly was instant attention. "Why didn't you put him through to me? I've been here all morning."

"Because he didn't ask to speak to you, Dr. McDonough. He asked me to tell you he'll be arriving back late this afternoon and that he'll be at your apartment sometime after eight."

"The hell he will!" Molly snapped. "I have other plans." That was a lie. She'd had absolutely no interest in dating since —

"If you value your job, you'll be there. Mr. Elliott is not a wise man to cross."

You stupid old witch, I don't value my job, and I've crossed James Elliott more times than he'd care to admit, Molly wanted to scream back at the smug, disapproving figure by the door. The only sign of her temper was the darkening of her blue eyes, and her voice took on added huskiness. "That's too bad," she said finally. "Because I'm not going to be there. And I won't be around tomorrow either. The brochure has to be in to the printers by 9:00 A.M. Monday morning, and that crucial list is missing. There's nothing I can do but leave immediately for the hacienda and recompile it."

"That's a five-hour drive!"

"Oh, don't worry about me, Ms Bateson. I'll be spending the weekend. Ever since I started reading about it, I've wanted to see it. I'm amazed I didn't think of it sooner. A weekend of solitude will be just the thing."

"But—but it isn't finished yet. It isn't ready for guests."

"Don't be absurd. I know the place better than you do by now. The workmen have been gone for a week. I'll just phone the security guard and let him know I'm coming."

"But there's no plumbing, no electricity—"

"If our scholars and tourists can rough it, so can I," Molly said breezily. "Tell Mr. Elliott I'm sorry I missed him, and that I'll see him again Monday morning. That is, if he hasn't decided to disappear again."

The smug hostility had vanished from Norma Bateson's pale face. "Dr. McDonough, I would strongly advise against driving down there tonight. For one thing, Mr. Elliott will be extremely displeased if you aren't around to consult with him, and for another, the weather is hardly conducive to long drives—"

"Thank you for your concern, Ms Bateson, but I've driven in worse weather. But I'll take off now so I don't have to drive much after dark. I'll see you Monday morning."

"But—" Molly was already out the door, her raincoat over one arm and her leather purse over the other, feeling quite pleased with herself.

Six and a half hours later she wasn't feeling quite so smug. The rain was coming down in sheets, had been since she left San Francisco a little after two, and visibility and traction on the highway were tenuous, to say the least. By the time she was heading toward the hacienda on the dimly lit secondary road they were almost nil, and the three-mile long winding road down the peninsula to the isolated hacienda was a sea of mud. Molly's Peugeot kept up its forward motion, but just barely, the wheels spinning sideways in a vain attempt at traction.

Her nervous hands clutched the steering wheel tightly, and beads of nervous sweat ran down between her breasts as she desperately tried to maneuver up the slippery ink-dark road. The last little bit of traction deserted her, the back wheels spun around, and she was sideways across the narrow mud track, the car stalled out, the headlights staring sightlessly into the pouring rain.

With shaking hands she restarted the engine and slowly, carefully, drove off to the side of the road. Turning off the car, she sat there for a long moment, trying to control the sudden trembling in her limbs. One thing was certain, she wasn't driving anywhere tonight—either on ahead to the hacienda or back to the small, seedy coastal town she had just driven through. The only way she was traveling was on foot. According to everything she had read, the hacienda couldn't be more than a mile up ahead, and Molly, when in training, could easily run that distance. However, at that moment she scarcely felt like crawling, much less running, and the only thing she was in training for was beating up James Elliott. And even that had proved a dismal failure.

Her high-heeled leather boots slid precariously in the mud as she climbed out of the car, but somehow she managed to remain upright. She blessed the foresight that had prompted her to change into old jeans and a sweater, and grabbed the knapsack filled with a change of clothes, several cans of soup, and various other instant foodstuffs. She'd been too angry to stop for food in the first place, and then too frightened by the treacherous weather, so that by now she was absolutely ravenous, as well as being wet, tired, angry, and just a little frightened. She started off down the road, her traction in the thin leather boots not much better than the radial tires of her car, and heartily cursed James Elliott and her own rash temper.

"One thing's for certain," she said to the pouring rain that practically obscured her vision. "They're going to have to do something about this road if they want the place to be accessible." The sound of her wry voice in the tempest proved immeasurably cheering, so she tried whistling as she struggled onward, the knapsack weighing down on her shoulders. Why hadn't she brought dried soup instead of heavy cans? And why hadn't she had enough sense to stay home, warm and dry, with James Elliott arriving at her doorstep in all his dangerous, infuriating glory?

The whistling sounded a trifle forlorn in the angry darkness, so she quickly changed to her good, clear soprano. "'Give me some men who are stouthearted men, who will fight for the right they adoooore...'" she bellowed into the windy night, so pleased with herself that she almost didn't notice when the adobe walls of the hacienda loomed up out of the blackness. She fell against the thick wooden door with a glad cry. "Oh, thank heavens," she murmured against the solid door. And then remembered that the keys were in her briefcase, a mile back in the mud.

The words of frustration and rage that rang through the night would have normally never escaped her lips except when goaded by James Elliott, and the door remained impassive to her furious poundings. Slipping the heavy knapsack from her shoulders, she mucked through the mud alongside the house and slammed it through the nearest window. The sound of breaking glass brought her out of her blind rage, and with great care she removed the jagged edges of glass from the shoulder-high window before boosting herself up and over, landing on her bottom on the hard tile floor. Shards of glass were all around her, but fate had finally decided to be kind. None were embedded in her bruised posterior.

It took only a moment or two to locate the knapsack and the still-working flashlight. She was in some sort of storeroom. Maybe fate would be kind enough to let her find a working fireplace and a nice, dry supply of wood in close proximity.

The fireplace was close at hand, taking up one wall of the huge main room of the hacienda. The dry firewood was there, along with kindling and even a supply of newspapers. What was missing were the matches.

By now Molly was racked with shudders from the cold. She stared at the cold dark fireplace, sat back on her heels, and burst into tears.

And it was there that James found her, some twenty minutes later, the tears still wet on her face.

Chapter Twenty-Two

The noise of the storm had effectively covered the sound of his rented car driving up the deep, rutted road, the rasp of his key in the lock, even the slam of the heavy front door. She looked up from her position of abject misery in front of the cold, dead fireplace to see him looming in the doorway, the light from his lantern flashlight illuminating his furious features. Before he had time to utter whatever scathing denunciation hovered on his lips, Molly let out a glad cry.

"James, thank God you're here!" she gasped, and hurtled herself across the room and into his arms, tears coming anew. His arms closed around her, holding her tight against the hard, wet strength of his body.

"Damn, Molly," he uttered thickly in her ear. "I ought to beat you. Do you realize how frightened I was when I saw your car off the road?" He brushed her hair away from her tear-damp face as the light swung crazily from the other hand that was still wrapped tightly around her. "Don't you ever do that again."

"Do what?" she murmured, reveling in the feel of his hard, comforting body around her.

"Drive straight into the worst storm in the last five years just to spite me."

"I didn't know it was that bad a storm," she whispered against his chest. "My car radio is broken."

"You don't deny you were trying to spite me?" Carefully he set the flashlight down on a nearby table so that he could draw her more closely against him.

"Of course not. But I didn't expect you to come after me."

"Didn't you?" His voice was skeptical. "I thought you knew me better than that. You should have known I'd come tearing after you the moment I heard you were gone. Thank heavens Norma Bateson is such an infernal snitch."

"She called you?"

"She called me. I caught an earlier flight to Santa Barbara so I wouldn't have as far to drive." He held her a little away from him, staring down at her up-turned face through the darkness. "Why didn't you expect me to come after you, Molly?"

"Because I don't know what to expect from you," she said in a low voice. "I never know what you're going to do next. When I expect to see you, you're gone. When I get used to—to not being around you, you show up."

"Like a bad penny?" he offered, his hands warm on her body. His mouth grazed her forehead lightly. "Or a homing pigeon?"

Misery welled up inside her at the touch of his lips. "I don't understand you!" she cried. "What do you want from me, James?"

"At this point I want to keep you confused and off guard," he said frankly, loosening his grip slightly.

"You do a very good job of that."

"And I'll let you know what else I want when I think you're ready to give it to me."

Molly's prosaic mind immediately went to the treasures that filled her apartment. "The Carolina lily quilt?" she hazarded. "Or my spool bed? If it's Sebastian's picture, you can forget it."

He released her with a small push, a disgusted tone in his voice. "How anyone can be so astute in some matters and so incredibly obtuse in others is beyond me. Why don't you have a fire going?"

Molly was still reeling from the abrupt withdrawal of his arms as much as from the change of subject. "I—I forgot to bring any matches," she confessed, and was rewarded with his sudden shout of laughter.

"I'm glad to see you too can be inept," he responded. "Did you bring any warm clothes? If so, you'd better change into them while I get this fire going. You're even wetter than I am."

"Can I borrow your flashlight?"

"What for?" he questioned irritably, already busy with the matches.

"So I can find a place to change," she shot back, annoyed. "My batteries are almost dead, or I'd take mine."

The paper in the fireplace caught, sending flickering shafts of light across James's face. "You can damn well change right here, or I'll do it for you. I'm not in the mood for any missishness."

"I'm not being missish!"

"Then don't be coy either," he snapped. The dry kindling had caught with a comforting crackle, and James took a deep breath. "Look, Molly, we're stuck here, at least for the night, so why don't we make the best of it? Truce?"

"I'm sorry," she said in a small voice. "I really appreciate your coming after me. I was terrified when I finally made it here. First I couldn't find the keys, and then when there weren't any matches, I panicked."

"You did very well," he said warmly, rising and turning from the fire. "I'm glad you had the sense to break that window. I hate to think of you wandering around..." His voice trailed off as he faced her.

She had moved to the far end of the room, hoping the shadows would hide her, and quickly stripped herself of her clothes. Her numbed fingers made dealing with the buttons tedious work, and she was standing there, barefoot, clad only in the thin, somewhat dry wisps of lacy lilac bikini panties and bra, when he turned and caught sight of her.

She was about to reach for her knapsack and the dry clothing when something stopped her hand. The flickering light from the fire illuminated her nearly nude body, the flames playing over her pale skin. Warmth was beginning to fill the room, although whether it was from the fire or James she couldn't really tell. An answering warmth filled her, and slowly, deliberately, she reached in front of her and undid the clasp of her bra, freeing her full breasts from their confines. Her breathing was coming more rapidly now as she dropped the bra to the floor with her other clothing. Her eyes never leaving his dark, intent ones, she slid her hands beneath her panties and began to slide them off, slowly, sensuously, a small, deliberate smile playing about her mouth.

"Aren't your clothes wet?" she questioned somewhat breathlessly, her voice huskier than usual.

In answer he pulled the heavy Norwegian sweater over his head, tossing it into the shadows, and one large hand moved to the buttons of his heavy flannel shirt. "I don't suppose you were farsighted enough to bring a sleeping bag?" He pulled the tails of his shirt from his jeans and slipped it off, tossing it after his sweater. His chest gleamed in the firelight, and it was all Molly could do to hide the wave of longing that washed over her body.

To cover the sudden surge of feeling she leaned down, catching up the sleeping bag and tossing it to him. "I'm not completely unprepared," she said lightly. "But I'm afraid it's only a single—I really wasn't expecting you."

"Oh, I believe you." He spread it out in front of the fire. Straightening back up, his hand moved to his belt, and his eyes met her large, longing ones as he slowly undid the buckle. His hand paused at the zipper of his jeans, and the scorching look he sent her was enough to melt her bones. "Are you being a tease tonight, Molly?" he asked, his breathing ragged.

Slowly she shook her head. "No, James. Are you?" She crossed the room to him, her bare feet silent on the cold stone floor, until she stood directly in front of him, her nude body reflecting the dancing flames.

Shadowed against the firelight, he towered over her,

large and dark and menacing. She couldn't see his expression, and it was better that way, she thought. "Make love to me, James?" It was a question, a plea, a tiny, polite request. In answer his hands reached out, caught her bare arms in a firm, gentle grip, and pulled her against his body.

"How could I help myself?" he murmured against her hair, drawing her down beside him on the thick down sleeping bag. And slowly, delicately, he began to do just that, his hands and fingers, his lips and tongue, loving her in the warm glow of the firelight.

She came alive beneath his touch, her body and soul and heart crying out for him, giving to him, holding nothing back. Again and again he brought her to the edge of completeness and beyond, until at last he joined them, and she clung to him in the storm, sobbing out her joy, as they rocked together in the timeless bonds of love. And when the tumult came for both of them, it came in a shower of stars. Her face was buried against the straining muscles of his neck, her arms clinging to him for safety in her storm-tossed world, as her mind cried out *I love you, I love you, I love you.* But her mouth was silent against his smooth warm skin as she rode the crest of the tempest till they anchored safely once more in the lee of the storm. And wrapped tight in the haven of his body, she slept.

Chapter Twenty-Three

She was running away again, and well she knew it. But this time she knew what she was running from. She was in love with James Elliott—there was no avoiding the awful truth any longer. She was so in love that it made anything she had ever felt before pale in comparison. And her only thought, as he'd told her before, was flight. She was a game for him, a challenge, someone to confuse and manipulate. Once he knew she loved him, the challenge would be gone, and she'd be left so shattered and broken that it could be next to impossible to build that safe, comfortable shell again.

That, of course, was the only answer to her plight, she thought as she struggled down the muddy road in the early morning sunlight. As soon as she got up the nerve she would tell him that he had won; that she loved him, would do anything for him, like the most abject idiot. That would end it. A quick, neat slice like the blade of a guillotine, and she could go back to the museum and Dr. Matheson's peculiarities and forget James Elliott the Fourth ever existed.

And she'd always have last night. Never would she try to erase that from her memory, no matter how painful it was to relive it. That was what love and making love was all about, that commitment of body and soul that went beyond a physical joining into realms so awesome that it almost frightened her. It was difficult to believe that he could have come to her again and again during the night, to share that wondrous commitment, and yet feel nothing more than animal attraction and a cynic's fascination for a challenge.

But that was all she could count on, and that wasn't enough. Not a word of love had passed his lips during the night, even though his actions shouted it, whispered it, sang of it. He was still sleeping soundly when she'd reluctantly crawled from the shelter of his arms, pulling on her clean clothes and sneaking out barefoot into the cool December morning. The storm had ended sometime during the night, and the sun sparkled off the mud. Molly's boots were ruined, but it was too cold to hike over a mile down the road in bare feet, so she pulled them on with a grimace. If she didn't move soon, she'd lose her nerve, run back, and burrow next to him in the sleeping bag, and she wasn't quite ready for that. She was too vulnerable. She needed to regain some tiny portion of her self-control before he destroyed it.

Her car was exactly where she had left it, just over a mile down the muddy road. It had seemed farther in the pouring rain, she thought as she climbed into the front seat. Really, she should have just curled up and spent the night in the car. A lot of trouble would have been saved.

A low wail of despair escaped her lips. The keys were gone. Desperately she racked her brain. Had she taken them with her last night? She was sure she had deliberately left them there, in case she was blocking the road for someone. How could she have been so stupid? They must be somewhere in the mud, and she'd never find them.

That left her with one alternative—James's car. Tempting as the thought might be, she quickly dismissed it. She couldn't do that to him again, she just couldn't. Perhaps if she got moving, she might make it to the highway before he woke up and found her gone. She'd never hitchhiked before, but there was always a first time for anything.

Her hand was on the door handle when she heard the sound of a car. The forlorn hope that it might be coming from town was quickly dashed as James's rental car rounded the corner and pulled up beside her. She remained where she was as he climbed out of the driver's seat and stalked around to her. For a moment she considered locking the car door, then abandoned it. A locked door wouldn't keep James Elliott out.

"Lose something?" he drawled, holding out her keys. His face was perfectly blank, not an emotion, not even anger marring the aloof, arrogant planes. "I took these last night when I drove in. I expected you to run off, and I thought I'd better be prepared." Leaning over, he dropped the keys in her lap.

She kept her eyes downcast, afraid to look up at him, afraid he'd read the love and longing in them. "I'm sorry," she said inadequately.

"For what? For proving me right again?" The cold

neutrality was worse than lashing rage. "Go ahead, Molly. Run away again. I'd just as soon not have to look at you for a while."

At that she did raise her head. "Does that mean I'm fired?"

"Don't be so hopeful. I'll expect you at the party Feinham's giving for Sebastian tonight."

"I don't want to go."

"I don't give a damn. You're going. I'll give you your choice of having me pick you up or meeting me there."

"I'll meet you there," she said, resigning herself to the inevitable. It would give her more time for the escape that was taking shape in the back of her mind. Greece would be beautiful this time of year.

"All right." She could read nothing in his tone but indifference. "If you're not there, I'll come and get you, Molly, and you won't like my temper if I do. And don't think you can hide from me, or run away if I really want to find you. You can't."

"Not with busybodies like Norma Bateson spying on me," she shot back.

A wry smile twisted his mouth. "You don't like Norma? I can't say as I blame you—she hates your guts."

"But why? I've never done anything to hurt her."

James looked at her for a long silent moment, and she flinched beneath his cool regard. "She's convinced you're bad for me," he said finally. "I'm not sure I don't agree." And without another word he turned his back on her, climbed into the driver's seat of his rented car, and with a minimum of effort turned the car around to head back to the hacienda.

It took Molly a great deal more effort to get the small Peugeot heading back toward town. Only her determination not to ask James for help enabled her to manage it, not without pushing, swearing, sweating, and shoving fallen branches under the spinning wheels.

San Francisco had never looked so good to her. She collapsed in her apartment, unplugging the telephone to keep out any unwelcome intrusion. A long, hot shower went a little way toward restoring her equilibrium, and a glass of sherry and a two-hour nap finished the job. When she awoke, her bedroom was dark, and she lay there, conscious only of a feeling of miraculous well-being. And then she remembered. She loved James Elliott. She found herself smiling into the darkness, sudden delight filling her and banishing the very last trace of panic.

With her newfound determination she could barely recognize the sniveling coward who had staggered in a few hours ago. She loved James Elliott, and she wasn't about to give up without a fight, and she wasn't about to run away anymore. She would move heaven and earth to make him love her in return, not admitting defeat until she was forced to. And then she'd fight some more. He'd told her he loved her once, and she hadn't believed him. But maybe he *had* meant it—maybe he really did love her already. With James Elliott there was no way to be sure of anything, not even defeat. And Molly had no intention of settling for anything less than total victory.

It was late, far later than she could have wished, and she would have to hurry if she was going to make it in time. The party was due to get under way by seven. If she didn't show up by eight, James would come after her—unless he decided she wasn't worth bothering about, which certainly wasn't outside the realm of possibilities.

The travel section of the Sunday paper was still spread out on her coffee table beside her empty sherry glass, and contemptuously she tossed it to one side. For once in her life she wasn't going to run. She was going to give James Elliott one good chance, and if he threw it away, he didn't deserve her. She didn't really deserve him, but then, fate wasn't fair, and she might just get lucky. She had so far.

Lucia was home to her hurried phone call, and enthusiastically agreeable, even promising to meet her at the museum in an hour. For a moment Molly considered it, then changed her mind. "No, thanks, darling. I'd better do it myself. Give Ian my love, and thank you."

"Ian sends you his love too. He wants to know when we can get married."

"Hmmm?" Molly was searching through the Yellow Pages and only listening with half an ear.

"I told him we couldn't get married until you were settled," Lucia explained with great patience. "He wants to know when that will be."

"Soon, I hope. I'll let you know tomorrow."

"You wretch! You'll call me tonight," Lucia demanded.

"I hope I'll be too busy to get to a telephone," Molly replied demurely. "Wish me luck."

"I do, darling. I do."

Late, late, late. She felt like the rabbit in *Alice's Adventures in Wonderland*. It had taken far longer at Colette's Lingerie than she had expected, and then the new guard at the museum had proved exceedingly difficult until he talked with Lucia on the telephone. Consequently it was a quarter past eight when Molly finally arrived at the Feinham Gallery, her cape wrapped tightly around her.

"There you are, Molly." Barry greeted her with a clanking of cheekbones. "People have been asking for you all evening."

"Who?" she demanded breathlessly.

"Sebastian, of course. And Jeremy Cabello's been sulking in the main room. I think he wants you to hold his hand and tell him he's better than Sebastian. And, of course, there's James Elliott. Why don't you give me your cape and I'll get rid of it."

"Of course, James Elliott," Molly murmured, still clinging to the wrap. "Where is he? Is he still here?"

"He's in the back room, looking at some older pieces. He was so busy glowering at everybody that I told him he was scaring away customers. Do you want me to get him for you?"

"Don't worry, I'll find him." She slipped the velvet cape off into his waiting hands, threading her way through the crowds toward the back room. As good a spot as any, she thought, ignoring the curious glances that followed her wake. If he had a sentimental bone in his cold, arrogant body, it could only work in her favor.

His back was to her when she appeared in the doorway. The painting he was staring at wasn't worth his attention, and without hesitation Molly cleared her throat.

Whirling around, he began angrily, "I had just about given up hope. You certainly took your time..." As his eyes focused on her appearance his voice trailed away for a moment. "But it was obviously worth the effort," he finished softly. "Where did you get that?"

She moved into the light, the Edwardian lace dress swirling around her ankles. "Off a lifeless dummy at the museum," she replied, hoping her nervousness wouldn't show. "I thought you approved of art for the living."

"I do, I do." That intent light had come back into his eyes, the light she was never sure she could read. "Aren't you afraid of shredding the material?"

"It's worth the risk."

"What is?" he demanded. "What made you change your mind about the dress? Doesn't it violate your sacred principles?" He wasn't making it easy for her, she thought with a pang.

"I thought I might meet you halfway," she said, and her voice was very quiet and sure in the still room. He continued to stare at her, making no response, and her palms began to sweat. "You said you'd tell me what you wanted from me. I'm ready to give you anything you want. I'm not going to run away anymore." The words came out with a little catch in her voice, and the pounding of her heart was deafening in her ears. He just continued to stare at her.

"Why?" The word was softly spoken, and she had no choice but to answer it.

"Because I'm in love with you."

For a long, aching moment that stretched into an eternity he said nothing. And then a brilliant, blinding smile lit his arrogant face. "In that case, dear heart, I want your body, your mind, your soul, your name, and everything else I can entice, seduce, or browbeat from you. I want to marry you and make love to you morning, noon, and night, and then when you're ready, I want to get you pregnant with our child. I want to live with you and work with you and fight with you for the rest of our lives."

"Me too," she whispered and went into his arms. His mouth met hers in a kiss of such soul-scorching proportions that they both drew back, a little frightened.

"Do we have to stay here?" she whispered huskily.

With a slow tender smile he shook his head, and Molly wondered how she could ever have thought he was arrogant. "We can go back to my apartment," he said. "On one condition."

"Name it."

"You tell me what in the world you're wearing under this dress."

She grinned up at him. "A lace corset and garters," she replied. "What else?"

"Oh, God."

"And the satin sheets are out in my car," she added with an impish smile.

His laugh rang out with hers. "What are we waiting for?" And his hand caught hers in a tight, loving grip. "Let's get out of here."

"Humph!" Henry Matheson fixed his milky blue eyes on the towering red-haired artist standing on the walkway leading up to James and Molly Elliott's hillside hideaway. "Surely you can't be invited to this christening? I wouldn't have thought being the mother's ex-lover would qualify you as a member of the family."

Sebastian cast a hurt expression down at the irascible old man, at the last moment remembering just how much the Museum of American Arts had spent on his paintings over the years. He managed a sad smile. "I don't suppose you'd believe I was little Elinor's godfather?"

"I don't suppose I would," Matheson grumbled. "That child is going to have enough trouble with parents who battle all the time the way James and Molly do."

"Don't you think they're happy?" Sebastian demanded with a ghoulish eagerness.

"Of course I do, you dolt! And a baby couldn't ask for better, more loving parents. I just don't imagine it will be particularly peaceful in the next few years." Matheson started up the steep stone steps that led to the absurdly modern and surprisingly comfortable redwood-and-stone house that overlooked the ocean. He sighed with anticipatory exhaustion. "I love this house, but I wish James had arranged for easier access. I'm getting too old to climb mountains, even to

visit James and Molly." He cast Sebastian a specula-
tive look. "Are you sure you're welcome?"

"Of course." Sebastian followed him, his affronted
expression lost to Matheson's narrow back. "Besides,
with James taking the next three months off from the
Seaquist Foundation, I'll be left high and dry. He was
supposed to accept delivery on several canvases—"

"For heaven's sake, man, you aren't planning to
talk business today, are you?" Matheson ignored the
fact that he was planning the same thing. Since James
and Molly had arranged to spend alternating three-
month periods taking care of their two-week-old
baby, he had the vague hope of enticing her back to
the museum and her old job, at least part-time. Up
until now she'd shown no inclination to leave Elliott's
side and the Seaquist Foundation's new museum
complex, but if Elliott was going to be at home with
the baby whenever she worked, it was just possible...

"What's keeping you?" Molly's voice floated down
the steep hillside, rich with good humor and happiness.
Matheson squinted up against the bright sunlight to see
her silhouetted against the starkly beautiful lines of the
house Elliott had designed for her. "Charles and Elinor
and the family have been here for almost an hour, and
the food's just about gone."

Matheson ignored the groan of anguish from the
hulking giant behind him. Molly's blond hair was a
luxuriant halo around her head, the small, wrinkled
form of her daughter was held safely in her arms, and
James Elliott loomed up behind her, a possessive
hand on her shoulder, his proud expression warring
with the faint suspicion that clouded his eyes as he

looked down at Matheson's determined features. Eighteen months of marriage and the birth of their first child definitely agreed with them, Matheson realized with a pang. It would be useless to even try to steal Molly back to work at the museum.

"We're coming," Matheson grumbled, abandoning the pitiful shuffle he had adopted to convince Molly of his need and bounding up the last few steps with a youthful vigor. "Don't be so impatient; you're not going anywhere."

Molly smiled serenely down at the child in her arms, leaning against her husband's shoulder. "No, I'm not," she agreed with a blissful sigh.

THE GOLDEN CAGE

The first Harlequin American Romance Premier Edition by bestselling author ANDREA DAVIDSON

Harlequin American Romance Premier Editions is an exciting new program of longer–384 pages!– romances. By our most popular Harlequin American Romance authors, these contemporary love stories have superb plots and true-to-life characters–trademarks of Harlequin American Romance.

The Golden Cage, set in modern-day Chicago, is the exciting and passionate romance about the very real dilemma of true love versus materialism, a beautifully written story that vividly portrays the contrast between the life-styles of the run-down West Side and the elegant North Shore.

Wherever paperback books are sold, or send your name, address and zip or postal code, along with a check or money order for $3.70 (includes 75¢ for postage and handling) payable to Harlequin Reader Service, to: Harlequin Reader Service

In the U.S.
Box 52040
Phoenix, AZ 85072-2040

In Canada
P.O. Box 2800, Postal Stn. A
5170 Yonge St., Willowdale, Ont. M2N 5T5